MICAELA'S BIG BAD

A HALLOWEEN NOVELLA

TIJ

For all the readers who love Halloween,
and a little bit of magic.

1

JAY HAPPENED

The only thing standing between me and me getting drunk was a naked four-year-old.

He was my best friend's nephew, and he was swinging his little penis in the air, staring at it, smiling and giggling, and clapping his hands with glee. He was also standing just inside the door, and I was standing on the doorstep, a full bottle of whiskey needing to be drank, and he wouldn't let me in.

"Heya, Bud."

More laughing.

He clapped.

He was shaking his little hips as if it were the first time he'd learned how to shake those hips.

"Bud."

That was actually his name.

"What?"

I nodded to the doorhandle. "Let me in."

"No." He hit the lock—shit, my hands were full, but why hadn't I just grabbed for the handle, anyway?—and took off running.

Crap.

I had a bulging backpack on me. Three grocery bags were hanging from one of my arms, the same one I had my coffee in. My other free hand held the whiskey. I knew my priorities. Also, the grocery bags were filled with my clothes, or at least what I had been able to grab in a desperate speed-round of packing.

I went so fast. If there was a speed packing race, I could've been a contender.

Not a winner, a contender. After all, I was realistic about my abilities.

The most extraordinary thing about me was my long hair. I had long dark hair.

Jay used to whisper how he liked to twine it in his hands when he—nope. Not going there.

But this was me. Micaela Nadeem, an energist who didn't use my energist side. Middle of the road. Some might say boring. I played everything safe. No risks in life. Not great at anything, but not bad at anything either.

Even leaving my boyfriend, I half-assed it. I took what I could, and bolted.

And I threw a fork.

I should've thrown a knife. At least a knife? Why not go totally lame and toss a spoon instead? Nope. A fork. I was a fork girl. A fork non-energist energist.

My car was full of blankets, what bathroom toiletries I'd been able to grab, and all my schoolwork, because this fork girl still needed to finish two courses before I had a bachelor's in communications. What I planned to do with that? I hadn't a clue. See my theme here.

I barely knew what I was going to do past tomorrow, so the future was totally up in the air.

I was not, what someone would call, a *planner*.

Who are those people?

They're a species I'll never understand.

I tried hitting the doorbell with my elbow.

Nothing. I chafed against the wall instead.

I tried a second time.

Rin—

It cut out.

Great.

I had two options. Put my stuff down, find my phone (I had no idea which bag I'd stuffed it in) and try her that way. Bud was here, so chances were high that Nikki was babysitting, but her phone always seemed off so the probability of that working was nil.

My other choice: "Nikki! *Nikki!* NIKKI!"

She came out from the back hallway, her shirt hanging down one arm, doing up her pants, and her hair was all frayed everywhere.

I—

I couldn't.

Not at all.

Her eyes went wide seeing me, and she cringed.

Her face was all red and splotchy.

Her lips swollen.

She came over, cursing under her breath, and unlocked the door. She opened the door, stepping back. I stepped in, and hissed under my own breath, "You just got laid! While you're babysitting!"

More cringing from her, but she shut both doors and swung around to me. "I—" She took in my bags, and surmised the contents in my bag, and her eyes got round all over again. "Oh no, Cale."

I wrinkled my nose at her. "Don't 'Cale' me in that tone. Babysitting. You! Bud locked the door on me."

"Bud?!" She whirled around.

And Bud decided to come running back down the hall, yelling at the top of his lungs, arms in the air. Still naked.

"Bud!" she gasped, rushing to him. "What are you doing here?"

She lunged right.

He jumped left.

She jumped left.

He dodged, then climbed up on a chair.

"BUD!"

Still giggling, he got up on the kitchen counter, and ran the length of it. He was fast approaching the point where he'd be caught or have to jump because across from him was the refrigerator.

I heard Nikki draw in a swift breath of air, at the exact same time as I held mine.

He launched—

"BU—"

He was caught mid-air by two muscular arms.

He was curled up to a very manly and shirtless chest, and he was carried the rest of the way into the living area where I was still standing, still holding all my bags, still clutching that whiskey because I was still hoping to crack this sucker open tonight and drown every last sorrow.

"Uncle Cream!" We were *still* on the high-pitched theme here. That was coming from Bud, and he was pulling with all his might at his Uncle Brad's hair.

There was a story behind why Brad was nicknamed Cream, but I never heard it—actually, I never wanted to hear it. I was hoping to go through my entire life not knowing...and now onto the weird family awkwardness here.

Brad and Nikki were not boyfriend/girlfriend, or at least I hadn't been updated on an official relationship status.

What they were, though, were siblings to Bud's parents.

Nikki's sister married Brad's brother, and their first shindig that resulted in my best friend having to do up her pants happened the night their siblings were married.

Do the math.

Bud was four.

Nikki's sister didn't get preggo until the honeymoon.

Brad ending up in Nikki's bed, on and off, had been going on for a long-ass time. I say it like that because there are always aftershocks whenever Brad comes around.

Then, he would leave.

Nikki had tried closing up the bedsheets to him, but he could charm and seduce her and say all the nice words to her to get those sheets back opened pretty much any time he deemed her worthy.

He'd hotfoot out, and Nikki would get a text from one of our other girls (we had a lot around town), and there'd be a picture of Brad curled around another girl.

They were back and forth so much, and it'd been going on for almost four years.

This wasn't my drama, but I was her best friend, and I was pulling the best friend card and admitting only to myself that I was tired of the Brad-drama. Also, not shocked that he'd bring Bud around when he was hooking up with Nikki. How he got Bud into the house without Nikki seeing him before the bed-capades was something I also didn't want to know all the details about because Nikki was all looking shocked at seeing her nephew naked.

And in her house.

"What's up, Nadeem?"

I grimaced. "Don't speak to me."

Uncle Cream was the most real-life version of someone who reminded me of Billy Hargrove from *Stranger Things*. The difference was that Uncle Cream had straight hair, not curly hair. That was it. He could've been his twin, both physically and personality wise.

"Brad," Nikki snapped, but my best friend wasn't paying much attention to her recent lay. She was back to looking at me. Studying my bags. Studying the booze in my hand.

She noticed before, but got distracted. She was back to noticing and she was figuring it out.

My best friend was catching up here.

"Jay?" she asked.

Nope. That most definitely wasn't a frog in my throat. And it hadn't doubled in size when I nodded back.

"Yeah," I rasped.

Another cringe from her, mixed with a pitying look. I hated the pitying look.

The frog just did a loud-ass *ribbit*.

I looked away, and shuffled back because I knew what was going to happen. She would herd Uncle Cream and Bud, no—she'd make sure Bud got clothes on first—and once they were gone, she'd take my whiskey from me. She'd go to the kitchen. She'd pull out some drink glasses, put in some of the nice cubed ice she always keeps on hand for me, and we'd pour ourselves a drink. After that, it'd either be a veg-out night, which I was now wondering how that phrase came about? Because we'd sit, talk, fill each other in, and we'd drink. Pizza would either get ordered, or we'd go the other way.

We'd drink. Talk. And decide we needed to go out.

It was Halloween, a night we both avoided because we were usually insulted by how humans viewed us, but... Jay happened.

2

SOMETHING SOMETHING

"HE WAS IN MID-THRUST?"

We were an hour into drinking, and Nikki jerked toward me, sloshing her drink on the way.

She didn't notice.

"Mid-thrust."

I'd relayed the story of how I came home early from work, heard the moaning and groaning from the bedroom, and thought Jay was watching porn. That was it. That's all I thought.

I should've known better.

I did know better. That was the thing.

I had found texts on his phone three months earlier.

Silly me, right? Stupid me, more likely.

"Four years, Nik."

She moaned with me. "I know. Four years."

Fuck.

Four *years*.

"He was my high school crush."

"He was. You liked him for so long."

I did.

I had.

"You were, like, pathetic about it too. Like, really, really pathetic about it."

"Uh..."

"You wrote him poems. You drew hearts with his name in them on all the desks you sat in. You'd stare at him in every class you both had. You were the water girl for the football team, and had a special bedazzled water bottle just for him."

"Um."

"It was pink, with his name in a circle."

"Okay—"

"You offered to drive him home all the time, and you didn't have a car. You started taking cooking lessons from his mom, and you don't cook. You're banned from your own kitchen by your landlord. Or you were, when you lived with him, I mean..."

An awkward silence.

Not for Nik, apparently.

She was only taking a breath.

And breath taken. "You used to slip him anonymous letters." She reached for her glass. It sloshed again. "I never told you, but Becca Harris saw you slip a letter into his locker one day."

"She did?"

"She did." She took a messy drink. It sloshed down her throat. "She told Jay it was from you."

She paused, frowning. Her head cocked to the side. "I never told you about that."

I gritted my teeth. "No. You certainly did *not*."

She was still frowning to herself. "I should've told you. There was a reason I didn't tell you." She went back to thinking. "I can't remember it now."

I wanted to growl at her.

Screw it. I did. I bared my teeth too.

She just laughed, finishing her drink.

Shoving her chair back, she stood. "I need another drink—OH MY GOD! I forgot it's Halloween tonight."

"Yeah...?"

She looked at the clock, then grabbed for her phone, and she screamed again. "I'm supposed to work tonight."

"What?! We never do anything on Halloween."

"No—" But she was off, racing to her bedroom.

She came back, still rushing, and grabbed the whiskey before hightailing once again. She yelled over her shoulder on the way, "Grab my glass and follow me. I'm late, and I can't be more late."

"What?"

But I did as she asked.

With my own drink topped off, I took the rest of hers. She was in the bathroom, her make-up scattered everywhere. I grabbed her glass, filling it.

Sitting on her bed, facing her in the bathroom, I gripped my glass tightly. "You said you'd work Halloween tonight?"

I have to stress how this was so not normal.

We didn't do Halloween.

Halloween was for humans, not for us. Not for those of us who were 'other' than just human.

They dressed up like us, and it was beyond insulting.

Contrary to everyone's opinion, we weren't 'sexy fill-in-the-blank' all the freaking time.

I watched Nikki finish her makeup (record time) and disappear into her closet. Literally. Nikki was a demon. Not all demons were equal in their powers, but Nik had been working on her teleportation lately. Which was whoa, you know? Teleportation is huge in our circles, and my girl was achieving it. Granted, she could only teleport five feet away, but that's something in my book.

She came back a second later in black leather pants and a black leather corset. Her hair was up and she whispered a few words. As she did, her hair started braiding itself. It wasn't something she always did, but only at times like this—when she was late for work.

Her powers were growing more and more.

Not all demons are naturals. When Nik started trying to braid her hair, the scrunchie just kept flying through the hair. There used to be injuries, of everyone in the room except her.

"Nik!"

"What?"

"Why are you working tonight?"

She worked at a nightclub. Bass. All kinds went there, meaning ours and theirs. The humans. It was known as one of the most exclusive clubs in the Western Hemisphere. (That's our speak, not humans.) Humans don't talk like that. They'd say it's one of the most exclusive clubs in the nation or something like that. They only cared about country borders, state lines, county rules. Not us. We paid attention to territory, and Bass was straight up the best on our side of the world.

Nikki had been working there for the last year, and her powers had been getting stronger ever since. It was also known as a demon bar, where most of the employees were demons. I used to question it at first, but when she seemed to have her power in check, I backed off.

Power corrupted, or tended to corrupt, and I didn't want to lose her.

She hadn't answered my question. Her mind was distracted, and I could feel her communicating with someone else. It was my thing. I could see, feel, and hear energy, and with Nik right now, her energy was spreading out from her, completely leaving the room we were in.

I shoved up. "Nik! I'm getting alarmed here."

She snapped back to our room, all her energy focusing back around her. "You didn't finish telling me about Jay."

"What?"

"Jay. We were mid-thrust. *He* was mid-thrust."

Right. Because that was important here.

My boyfriend whom I'd known all my life, crushed on all through high school, had finally gotten together the last summer before college and had been living with the last two years, had cheated on me. At this point, I was more distracted why she was panicked about missing work tonight.

Her energy was off. Way off and it had turned on a dime.

There was a layer underneath that I'd never seen before. It was dark and swirly, and it surrounded her completely. It was clinging tightly to her body too. Nik's energy was never that tight usually. It usually just circled her like a fun-loving mist, and she had lots of pastel and sparkly colors intermixed. Good time Nik, almost always happy and content.

Actually, for a demon, she was all about the happy joy joy, you know?

I rattled off, "Jay was in mid-thrust into some vampire. It's whatever. I threw a fork at him, then a picture. And a few more pictures. I might've ripped down his favorite painting. I said a lot of shit, packed my bags, and I showed up at your place to get drunk."

She was putting on her heels.

Her clutch was next.

She was looking around.

Her phone was on the nightstand.

She grabbed it, and she was heading for the door. She had asked me to finish, and now was so distracted that it was insulting, "Then what?"

She reached for the door, but I was there.

I slapped a hand on it, knowing my eyes were hard when her head snapped up.

I spoke through my gritted teeth, "We stay in on Halloween. I left Jay. I'm your number one, and you're worked up about going to work, on a night you never work, and you know Benji would let you off." Benji was Bass' night manager, and he loved me. Well, he loved my cousin, but he adored me in a doting sort of way. He'd melt if I told him about Jay. "There's a rumor that a Big Bad is coming to town tonight."

I said town, but I meant city. We weren't too far from downtown Minneapolis.

And I wasn't lying about the Big Bad, but I *was* lying about the rumor.

I knew there was someone big and powerful coming to town. I'd been feeling his energy. Or her. I didn't discriminate except this energy felt masculine. Very, very masculine. Whoever it was had massive powerful energy that was already spreading to where we were. It was in the air.

"There's also a rumor that the new owner of Bass is making a visit tonight too. That got anything to do with you going to work on a night when we've made sure we don't work since we've both been born?"

I wasn't lying about that rumor. I heard it three days ago at a family picnic. The previous owner was a demon that got dead so Bass was sold, but no one knew who it was sold to. Everyone wanted to know who. Vamps. Werewolves. Witches. Demons. Other beings like me...well, except not me. I hadn't given two fucks who the new owner was.

That all changed now.

It's the only thing that made sense, and as soon as I said those words, that dark, swirly energy around her spiked. It doubled in size, and it was swinging around her head in a frenzied way.

I hoped that I'd been wrong. The evidence before me was telling me that I wasn't.

Nikki didn't answer. She closed her eyes, and I saw all her

energy morphing and starting to swirl around her, almost in a protective way.

She was going to teleport.

Away from me.

Me!

This was not like Nikki, not at all. Something was definitely off.

What the hell?

So...

Well.

I did something.

I had to.

I had done it once. The results had been disastrous, so I never did it again.

But I had no choice right now.

So I did what I did.

I grabbed her energy and I took hold.

She started to teleport, and—well, if I'd taken enough and held on, I would've too.

I only took a little, enough to ground her so she couldn't teleport. That, and she wasn't strong enough to teleport with me yet either.

When she didn't go anywhere, she sucked in her breath. Her head twisted to me. Her eyes flashed black, and she shoved me away from her.

She hissed, "This is a demon thing. Stay in your lane."

I relented and let her go, and she was off...but I knew three things.

One, that wasn't my best friend. Or that wasn't the best friend I loved.

Two, I should've been way more active in doing whatever I could've when she started working there.

And three, I didn't give a rat's ass about her lane, my lane. We were on this trip together.

I was going to Bass.

I looked around the room, seeing she'd left her glass untouched, and I headed over.

I might need a little something something to soften the edge because damn, humans on Halloween were annoying.

I drank hers. Mine.

I grabbed the rest of the bottle and headed out.

3

THANK YOU. JEEZ

I was walking down the highway when my Uber pulled up.

The front window rolled down, and the driver leaned over.

"You can't bring that in here." His bald head was shinier than normal, and the cross he was wearing swung toward me. It fell out of his sweatsuit, and not just any sweatsuit. This driver was wearing a red velvet sweatsuit.

Someone had aspirations to be a pimp. I wasn't stereotyping pimps. He'd actually told me this was his goal in life on another day when I had almost a full bourbon bottle with me.

I looked at my current bottle. There was a third left.

We non-humans could put the booze away and still function quite efficiently. I believe it's what you all call a high-tolerance level. Ours was epic.

I held it up and leaned down to look at the driver. "Come on, Ralph."

He shook his head. "Can't do it. I got my boss breathing down my neck as it is—"

"Take me to Bass," and I shook the bottle and its contents at him, "and what's left of it is yours—"

"Why are you still standing out there? Get in, Caley Girl!"

That was easy.

I slid in the back, and groaned when I smelled what I smelled. That stuff was not legal in Minnesota. "Really? You bust my balls over my booze?"

He shrugged, lifting up his joint for a drag. "Don't tell on me."

I groaned, leaning back as he took off into traffic.

Normally, this was bad. Very bad. Normally, I'd never allow myself or a driver under the influence to drive, but Ralph was different. I was different (well, I was being responsible. I ordered the Uber.) I knew Ralph toked up daily, so that was like him popping a cough drop. If he didn't, his throat would start getting scratchy.

"Why you going to Bass?"

"Nik's working."

He looked at me in the rearview mirror. "Why you going to Bass *tonight?*"

"'Cause *Nik's* working."

He was staring at me.

I was staring back.

Good thing we were at a red light.

That's when I knew.

I leaned forward, folding my arms over my knees and tucking my chin on the shoulder rest of the passenger seat. "You been feeling it too, haven't you?"

He pffted. "I don't know what you're talking about."

The light turned green, and he started forward, breaking our stare-off.

But I knew, and now he knew that I knew that he knew.

"What do you know, Ralph?"

We non-humans liked to use services from other non-humans. Because of this, our circle wasn't actually that small, but it felt small. Hence why I had called Ralph of all the drivers I knew, and I knew a lot. I mean, I grew up here.

I also knew Ralph knew because Ralph was like me. Except he wasn't.

It's confusing, I know.

"I don't know anything, Micaela."

I rolled my eyes. "Don't use my full name, Ralphianetterson."

Yes. That was his full name.

He stiffened.

"Tell me."

He cursed, hitting the turn signal and easing into the exit lane. "You shouldn't be going to Bass tonight, Caley Girl."

I relaxed. I *really* didn't like when someone used my full name.

I said quietly, "Why, Ralph?"

A small sigh from him as he eased into the right turning lane. "Does there have to be a reason? It's Hallo-fucking-ween tonight. That shit's enough."

"Why you driving?"

"Because I'm being *selective* tonight."

Meaning he was only picking up females. He had to pick me up. Cousins.

I tried again, "What do you know? Just tell me."

"I know what you know."

"And that's what? I just sense a Big Bad in town."

His eyes flicked up to mine. "And yet you're still going to Bass?"

Enough said.

Ralph and I were both energy sensors. That also meant we were energy magnets. Where we went, whoever's energy was around us, some of it stuck to us. Good and bad energy. I actively fought against that. I never wanted to take someone's energy. Too much and that was a drunk level that I never wanted to feel the hangover from. Some energy sensors never came back from it. They got addicted to it...and liked to keep rolling and rolling. Scary shit could take you over if you let it.

The other problem with that is that we were like drugs to other beings.

They liked to snack on us, in whatever way their species called for them to do, and they got a buzz from us. Blood. Sex. Just sniffing. Other ways. So we were like walking cocaine to some. To most not, but it was enough of a problem that we knew how to watch our backs.

This was another reason why I kept as little energy on me as I could. Self-preservation.

And going to where a Big Bad was going to be, not a smart move on my part.

"Nik's caught up in something."

"That's Nik's problem."

"Ralph."

"Caley Girl."

Have I mentioned that we're related? No? We are. See our similarities.

I sighed, looking out the window. We were nearing Bass. I didn't need to see the downtown section. I could feel the guy's energy. It was filling every alley we passed, covering every side-walk. Humans were happily walking through it, not a clue what was sweltering around them.

As we drew nearer to Bass, I felt a tickling inside of me.

It started at the base of my spine.

It was light, but there. It was almost grazing against me, softly. Sensually.

I didn't like that.

The Big Bad felt me coming; he was welcoming me.

"Cale, I really don't like you going there."

Ralph wasn't looking at me anymore. The traffic was almost

bumper to bumper and we had slowed to a snail's pace. Humans in costumes were walking up and down the streets, but he wasn't looking at them either.

He was seeing the energy. It was like a black mist that blanketed everything. Black with a tint of shiny metallic blue to it, and it was moving just as slowly as we were.

As we inched forward, it went with us.

Then it was moving toward us.

Then circling the car.

Ralph swore. "That's it. I'm not taking you. Can't even see to drive." He leaned forward, his hands clenching the steering wheel. "Move! She can't come if I can't see!"

The energy parted, but it moved up and over the car.

There was a whole rolling movement under the energy, and the blue mist's spark was even shinier beneath.

I swallowed over a lump in my throat. "You ever see something like that?"

Ralph had ten years on me. He was the elder and had seen a helluva lot more weird shit in his years than I had.

I wasn't sure that meant he was the smarter one...

He replied, just as in awe, but not a good awe, "No. I don't like that either."

"Me neither."

But I was still going to Bass even if I had to walk there.

Best-friend-combat ready, here I am.

BASS' entire building was shrouded over by the black energy mist. It was thick, and strong. Ralph pulled up to the front and leaned over to get a better view of it, and said under his breath, "That's pretty damn intense."

It was. Not in a good way.

He glanced back at me. "You sure I can't drive you away? Drop you off at your mom's and you can spend the night safe?"

I gave him a grim look, my insides just as grim and locked tight. "I gotta go in, Ralphie—"

"Don't call me Ralphie."

"—I gotta do it. For Nik."

We stared at each other again.

He nodded.

I nodded.

He said, "Don't do it for Nik."

"I hear you. I'm going in. For Nik."

"That's not what I'm saying. I'm saying—"

I was already out of the car.

"Hey!"

Right. I forgot.

I turned back and handed him the leftover whiskey.

"Thank you. Jeez."

Now I was off.

4

SQUEAK, SPLASH

RALPH ZOOMED OFF, and I turned to face the entrance to Bass.
The dark energy shifted aside, clearing a path for me.

Again, I have to reiterate how not normal this was. Beings,
non-human and human, weren't aware of their own energy or
their auras. I could see, feel, taste, touch, and smell all of that. It
was like a guidemap of the person. (I'm being gracious with this
use of the word.) I knew how they felt, what they were thinking,
or an indicator of what they were thinking. I knew all their past
struggles, their trauma, their after-life issues even. With non-
human beings, I knew what they were. I knew their powers. I
knew before they did a move, sometimes before they even
thought about doing the move.

Course, I kept my mouth shut about all of this.

All energy sensors did. Not just because of the whole 'drug'
thing we had going on, but because in the past, we were used as
weapons in warfare. There was a huge vampire/werewolf war
years ago, and our kind had almost been wiped out. One of the
remaining kids decided to shut up about letting others know
about our powers and what we could do, and that started a trend.

Shutting up.

Because of that, our kind started to grow again.

I came from a family of thirty family members in our local area. That wasn't counting the extended family members, or the extended, extended family members.

Because of all of that, and our history, I did what my ancestors did.

I shut up, kept my head down, and trudged forward into Bass.

"Heya, Nadeem."

I lifted my head up, giving a grunt as a greeting to Terath. He was one of the bouncers, and he was one of my cousins. He wasn't a sensor, though. He married into the family, but he knew all the secrets.

"You sure you should be here?"

See.

Another grunt was my response, and him knowing how I was, he sighed and opened the door for me. "Don't get dead."

A third grunt. But it was so true.

Once inside, the energy was better.

I wasn't even going to try to figure that out, because it should be thicker inside. Inside, I saw sexy goblins, sexy nurses, sexy vampires, sexy werewolves, sexy iguanas, sexy—everything. Wait. A girl had a cow costume on, with the udders hanging out in front of her, but the general costume wasn't sexy. Just the udder part.

Moving on.

I veered over to the bar and grabbed the first open standing area I found.

Leaning over and looking from one end to the other, I saw two bartenders and I had to stifle a curse because they were bartenders I didn't like. Both demons. And not Nik.

One saw me and came over, a mean glint in his eye. "Surprised you're here tonight." He reached for a glass.

I opened my mouth. I wasn't here to drink.

He poured me a martini, and well, he was done before I could protest.

He slid it over, dark humor mingling with that mean glint.

The mean glint was always there, because he was a demon. I was trying not to let my hackles get worked up about it, but this was Trey and that was hard to do. He was a cocky asshole on a good day, which said a lot for him being a demon. That basically said he was a good guy.

"On the house if you drink it and leave when you're done."

There were so many loopholes with that one. I took it and looked around. "There's a lot of humans in here."

"We cater to humans too."

I gave him a look. There were more than the normal amount they usually let in.

He indicated my drink. "Drink, then go."

Yeah, yeah.

I would drink it, and when I was *done* with why I came here, *then* I would leave. Easy-peasy. Contract fulfilled.

Trey narrowed his eyes, suspicion pinching his eyebrows together as I took my drink and stepped backwards. I was hoping to vanish into the crowd, like actually vanish, but I didn't have that type of power. Well, not without—never mind.

So, I had a drink. Point given.

I didn't know where Nik was. Point taken away.

I moved through the club, keeping to humans. They were drunk and annoying, but they didn't want to potentially use me— a guy's hand fell to my ass at that moment and he curved his body around mine. His mouth came to my ear right as he squeezed me. "Hey, baby. How you doi—"

I switched my drink to my other hand, reached up, and grabbed his wrist.

I slid a thumb over his artery, and he paused. I felt his swift intake of breath, and saw the excitement spike in his energy.

I took a firm hold of his wrist and wrenched it.

A startled and strangled scream erupted from him, and his body fell away from me.

He went to his knees, cradling his arm, and he gaped at me with tears in his eyes. "You—you broke my wrist, you bitch!"

Ugh.

Maybe I wouldn't hide among the humans after all.

I didn't respond to him, just lifted my drink for a sip and kept on moving. He had two friends with him, so I was eyeing both, but they only went to his side. One jostled into his side, and a second scream came from him.

His buddies were drunk. One girl with their group was staring at the broken-wrist guy in shock. Her eyes were wide and blinking, before she transferred her gaze to me. More blinking. Eyes still just as big, and she shook her head before she went over to his side.

I moved farther away, slipping around another wave of humans. Then, a second.

I couldn't see Nik anywhere on the first floor. I couldn't sense her energy either. That meant she was in an upper level, and that meant more security.

Just as I was heading for one of the stairs, I felt a shift in the air and glanced back.

The broken-wrist guy was standing and pointing to me. Two of the security guards were with him. One I knew. He was a demon, and like Trey, he didn't like me either. His eyes shuddered black for a bit.

Crap. That wasn't a good sign.

Also, there were a lot of demons here too. I was seeing way more than the normal amount for them.

Trey reached for his radio, and yep, totally needed to hurry my ass along. I didn't have time to be Veronica Mars.

I was moving along one of the back hallways, going from the

second-floor bar to the third level when suddenly that black energy from outside engulfed me.

A hand gripped my arm.

I had a moment's notice to give a squeak, see my drink splash, and I was dragged into a room.

Not good. Not good at all.

5

_____

WHO'S THE BIG BAD?

"What are you doing here?"

I recognized Nik's hiss, and relaxed. Fuck, I thought the Big Bad had gotten me.

We were in a janitor's closet, and I felt for the light switch. Turning it on, I looked down first.

My drink was okay. I only lost a little bit of it.

I looked and saw my best friend in full demon mode.

"Whoa."

I hadn't seen her like this, ever.

"What?" She retracted her hand and stepped back. She began patting herself. "What?"

"You got your horns out."

"What?!" Her hands flew to her head and she began feeling through her hair.

I was tempted to watch her keep feeling around before she figured it out, but also, she should know. The horns aren't literal, but the shadows of the demon's horn show when they're feeling all-demony.

I'd never seen her horns' shadows come out to play.

She kept patting, panicked, and I took pity.

"Stop." I reached for her hand, pulling it down. "You know just the shadows show. You don't actually grow horns while you're up here."

"Oh, yeah." Her relief was audible. "Thank Go—I mean. Whatever." She growled, remembering. "What are you doing here?"

"I'm here for you."

"Why?"

"Why?! Are you kidding?"

The black energy was attached to her, and it rose upwards, moving to her face.

The hairs on the back of my neck stood up. A shiver went down my spine. Why did I get a feeling the energy was staring at me, like it could actually see me? That had never happened.

I broke out into a cold sweat.

"You've got the Big Bad's energy all around you." I paused, watching her to see her reaction.

There was no shock. She only eased away from me an inch. Her eyebrows dipped down. "So? I'm working the room that he's in."

He. I'd been right.

Also, I had a fifty-fifty shot there, so I didn't know why I was rejoicing.

She eased away even farther, crossing her arms over her chest. "You shouldn't be here, especially tonight."

"Yeah, I've been told that a time or two on my way here. I'll leave if you leave with me."

"I'm working. This is my job."

Alarm was racing up and down my back, intertwining with those shivers like little snakes.

"You can get off work, and you know it."

All I needed was to call Benji. He'd let her off in a second if I asked.

"Benji's not here." She must've been reading my thoughts.

"Why? What do you mean?"

"He was fired last week."

"What?"

This was a whole new level of apocalypse. Benji fired? He was my go-to with all things Bass. After him, I had no connections here. Nikki and Terath didn't have any managerial power. Not that I normally cared about that stuff, but all the alarms going off in me were for something.

"I don't know. There's a lot of staff changes around here, and I don't get involved. It's a hazard to me."

My eyeballs almost popped out of my head at that. "Right there. That's a good enough reason. Come with me."

She laughed, easing away even more. As she did, the black energy doubled in size.

I was losing her.

She said, "I'm good. You're seeing something that's not there."

That was my daily life. Hello.

But that energy was swirling more and more around her. The same metallic sparkly undertones were there too. It was almost mesmerizing to watch. Under normal circumstances, I'd think it was beautiful to see. Not under these circumstances. And definitely not on Halloween.

"Nik, please."

"No." She was sharper this time. "Go home, Cale. You hate Halloween anyway."

I'd left my boyfriend of four years tonight, and I was pleading with her to leave with me. She wasn't acknowledging any of this. This was so not my Nik. No way, but I couldn't make her leave.

Well.

I could.

She just wouldn't be happy about it, and it wouldn't be permanent.

I could poof her somewhere. Then I'd have to try to knock her out.

But she was a demon, and Nik was strong.

I'd have to tie her up somewhere, I guess.

How could I tie her up where she couldn't just teleport out? I got it.

There were ropes I could use. They were used for angels, so... it'd do the job, but it would hella hurt.

Oh man. I didn't know what to do.

I feel like Ralph would know what to do.

"Who's the Big Bad?"

"What?"

"The Big Bad. Who is it?"

Her eyes flashed black again. The horns came out, and the whole room shook.

A weird sensation took root in my gut, and it began to build.

I wondered...

Fuck it.

I had to try. I had to know.

I grabbed her neck, my hand wrapping around it, and I shoved her up against the wall behind her. My movement was fast and violent, and I had a second before she'd rally back. I closed my eyes, head down, and I sensed into her energy.

I sensed everywhere.

In all circles of her energy. The Big Bad's energy.

Even the energy inside of her, and that's when I felt her. The real Nik.

She was there.

She was sleeping.

She wasn't in control of her body.

Suddenly, a whoosh happened and I was flung backwards.

I opened my eyes in time to see we were in mid-air. Nik's body was being thrown back against the wall. I was moving away from her, in the air, and I'd be crashing against the door any second. The energy had swirled up, becoming a solid force around her.

I heard its snarling.

I felt its anger.

But I also felt its power, and more importantly, I felt branded by it.

I knew in that moment I'd never feel anything more powerful.

Then, everything went dark.

6

THE BIG BAD

I woke up in a blue velvet room.

I was on a blue velvet couch. The walls were blue velvet. The ceiling. I couldn't find a door, so I'm sure that was blue velvet too. There were other chairs around the room, blue velvet on the arm rests. The floor was dark paneling, with blue and gold accents.

I lifted my head, and the whole room started spinning around.

I laid back down and took a second.

There'd be no escape action happening if I couldn't even stand.

Okay.

I waited, eyes open, and slowly the room stopped around me.

Scooting my legs over the edge, I sat up and waited. Holding my breath.

The room stayed put. Thankfully.

A low chuckle came from the dark corner of the room. "For an energist, you bounce back remarkably fast."

My eyes almost popped out. Again.

All the shivers and warnings from earlier slammed back into

my body as if they'd been there and had been trapped, the lid just now being lifted up. They filled every inch of my body, and I had a hard time staying upright.

I couldn't see him—holy shitballs, I couldn't see him!

His energy wasn't in the room.

Who could do that?

I mean, other than a Big Bad?

Okay. Could I get an energy concussion? Maybe that was it, I was now wondering. This was new territory for me. I ran when guys like him showed up, not that I'd come across anyone as powerful as him before, but still, I ran.

I was rambling.

I had to stop.

"Who are you?"

He stood from a chair. He was still in the shadows, but he was tall. Over six feet. And he was coming toward me.

My internal alarm was rising, rising. I felt it starting to choke me.

"You're unschooled for your power. That's a very stupid thing to do."

Oh. Fuck him. Lecturing me?

He stepped out of the shadows and all my words and snarky replies dried up.

Thought left me.

I—I was stunned speechless at the same time as an inferno was lit instead. It engulfed everything else. A full bonfire was raging in me. Flames and smoke must've been coming out of my head because this guy was like no one I'd ever seen. In movies or real life.

He was beautiful.

Almost too beautiful.

A five o'clock shadow peppered his face, and that jaw was the definition of a square jaw. His eyes were dark and smoldering.

He had a dimpled chin. His mouth—I licked my lips, my gaze going there and lingering and I was already daydreaming about nipping at his lips. They were perfect. He had a rectangular-shaped face, where there was a faint line from his cheeks dipping all the way to his jawline.

His hair was black, and it was short on the sides and there was enough on the top to have a good wave through it. A small lock fell down over his forehead, and I couldn't decide if it was either the hottest thing I'd seen or the most adorable.

With how he looked, though, I was leaning more toward dead sexy.

That phrase took on a whole different meaning for me, and I wasn't human. That said a lot.

He had broad shoulders, and a tapered waist. He was lean except for his chest and shoulders. There was something animal-like about how he moved toward me.

He was a shifter.

Not all shifters had the innate vibe he was giving out. It was exuding off him.

All authority and danger.

Power.

This guy, whoever he was, could snap his fingers and I'd be dust. I knew that without a doubt.

I also knew that this was the Big Bad.

"Who are you?"

Those eyes never wavered from mine, only narrowed, and he gave a small chuckle. The sound reverberated inside of me, warming and rubbing up against all of my organs at once.

"You come to my club. You accost my customers. And you try to get one of my employees fired. I believe you're in the wrong position here." He paused, his eyes becoming even more fierce. "You don't get to interrogate me."

That blaze in me sparked again, this time from irritation.

I liked to drink, spend time with my best friend, mostly avoid my family, and every now and then show up at my own job. What I didn't like was being told what not to do from someone I didn't know, and especially someone who was wreaking havoc with all of my senses.

I narrowed my eyes right back at him. "You don't feel like a demon."

It felt like I had to pull my gaze from cement as I took in the rest of him. He wore a business suit, tie off, top two buttons undone. The ends were pulled out of his pants, and he looked as if he'd raked his hand through his hair a couple times. It was messed up on top. As I was studying him, he took off the suit jacket and tossed it aside.

I watched in slow motion the whole muscle ripple effect that happened across his shoulders and chest.

That freaking frog was back in my throat.

He looked back at me.

I felt his disapproval in the air, almost singeing me, and I stomped down a growl.

I was getting tired of the ping-pong match of emotions and everything happening with this guy. He was too much for me. His power was coming off him in waves, even though he had checked his energy so it wasn't in the room with him. And how he did that, I had no clue. I'd never met anyone who could control their energy.

The way he was affecting me was overwhelming.

He only smirked. No answer.

"This is a demon bar."

He raised an eyebrow, his hand going to undo one of his cufflinks.

The other cufflink.

Holy.

I never knew I could be attracted to hands.

But I was. His.

They were man hands. Strong. Masculine. Firm.

"So that would make you a demon."

I was guessing here, hoping he'd confirm or deny.

Once both cufflinks were undone, he began rolling up the sleeves, showing a good length of masculine arms.

I was dying. Dying!

I'd never reacted like this to anyone.

Someone could roast marshmallows on my skin.

Wait.

Nik!

I forgot about Nik.

"Where's my friend?"

He paused at my question, his eyes unblinking for a moment before he turned, and now I was getting a bird's-eye view of the back of him. My mouth dried up all over again. The frog was dead. Evaporated. He was still rolling up those sleeves, causing the shirt to tighten over his back muscles. I was seeing the move and glide of all of those inches of man right before me.

Nik.

I needed to stay on track.

"My friend." My voice was a lot more authoritarian. "If you've harmed her—"

"What?" He turned at that. "What will you do if I've harmed your friend?"

I had to think.

The buzzing emanating off him was still so loud and so much of a distraction. I fought through, focusing. What would I do?

My power was energy, and he had none around him.

My Lord. That's why he didn't have his energy in here.

I was completely helpless to him.

When I didn't say anything, he turned back. "That's what I thought—"

He didn't finish that statement, and now I was pissed.

I stood, intending to go right for the door. I was looking all around and still hadn't found the exit, but I was hoping to pull off a miracle somehow when he looked back at me again.

An unseeing force slammed me against the wall.

I was raised in the air and held there, suspended. Helpless.

My arms were splayed out. Even my fingers were spread wide. My legs apart.

I was totally and completely vulnerable.

He asked, his tone mocking again, "What did you say you'd do?"

7

RIBBIT!

YOU'RE AN ASSHOLE.

Yes. I am. His voice came to me in my head, and I jerked at the intruder, shocked.

I mean, I couldn't jerk far, but my head did move a centimeter to the side.

His head was lowered, and the whole smoldering bedroom effect was happening with his eyes.

He spoke again in my head. *I've been sensing you, and I can't discern what you are.*

I'm an energy sensor. Duh.

No.

I froze. I mean, I froze more, or I would've if I could've moved.

What do you mean?

I can taste your fear.

That's disgusting.

You're scared of your own power. That intrigues me.

He moved closer to me, his head cocked to the side and his eyes turned almost soft. This was why I was reacting so much to him. He was inside of me, sensing me, studying me, dissecting me.

I felt violated. And not in a good way.

You're more than just an energy sensor. You have a unique taste that other energist's don't.

That blew wide open a whole new level of uncomfortableness. He was tasting me?

There's an ancient power in you. Maybe you don't even realize it, but I do.

Abruptly, as if he discovered something he didn't like, he withdrew. Everything. My insides were no longer cast in a throbbing inferno, and I fell from the wall. Landing, I caught myself, my elbow banging into the wall.

Damn. It was the same elbow I chafed at Nikki's too.

I felt way more orientated now and not as embarrassed.

I glared at him. "You didn't have to do all of that."

He gave me a cocky quirk of his top lip, but his eyes were cold. "You are in a building that is filled with demons on a dissension night where four of the six masters are rising."

Cold dread started to trickle in, filling the void that had been left by him.

I gulped.

I hadn't known it was a dissension night. They only happened once every six years.

He kept on, "Your kind has a long history of being taken as personal weapons...or worse. I would be very careful about how many insults you cast my way because your friend is gone. The demon has taken hold of her tonight, and I am the only thing powerful enough to get you out of here. Alive."

Dissension night was a night where the full moon was directly above us. And he was right. Every single demon lost their humanity, but what was worse was that it was also the night their masters surfaced and were given presents by their servants.

Every single demon had a master. There were six total, and the type of presents given?

There was a reason this place was filled with humans.

RIBBIT!

The frog was back, and the frog was shitting itself.

"Why would you help me?"

He was the Big Bad. That went against all universal and species' laws.

He gave me another scornful look, and I thought I saw him flick his eyes upwards. Actually, I was sure I did.

I had no idea.

I felt like he did.

I would've if I were him.

But his face was back to the same stoic mask from when he'd been analyzing me only moments ago.

"Do you have any other option right now?"

"You could be lying." I raised my chin up. "I could call your bluff, walk out there, and there's no dissension happening."

"Your friend would still be sleeping inside of her body."

Right.

Because that happened before he showed up on the scene.

Damn.

"What's the plan, Jeeves?"

He frowned. "Don't call me Jeeves."

"What's your name? I could call you that."

His eyes narrowed at me. They were pretty much staying that way.

He gave me one more long and measured look before there was a beep behind him. He walked to a panel in the wall and pressed it. A back door swung open (that was where it was! It was covered in blue velvet so it was camouflaged. Also, there was no doorknob.) and a female walked in who could've been a supermodel. Long legs. Thin body. High cheekbones. Disdainful eyes.

Vampire.

(The ones who look that beautiful and that disdainful were always vampires.)

They were staring at each other, and I knew she was telepathically reporting on something.

He gave a small nod, and she turned right back around. I got the coldest glance ever before she was through the velvet door. It swung shut right behind her, and before my eyes, the blue velvet smoothed over. The door completely blended in again.

"You had a witch do that."

After he pulled out his phone and was looking at the screen, he glanced up at me as I moved closer to inspect where the wall had been.

That was when I realized the room we'd been in was large. I'd been so focused on him that I hadn't even noticed my surroundings save for all the blue velvet.

He'd been clear across it for most of our little interrogation, until now.

I closed the space and was within five feet of him to look for the door the vampire had just exited.

Trying to focus on the door, I couldn't. I was assaulted by waves of his power. It was exuding from him, over and over again. Like it was pulsating from him, but wait. I turned and trained my eyes and my mind to look at him in a different way.

His power *was* pulsating from him.

Over and over again.

That's how he was shifting so his energy was never on him, but I could see the waves now, and it was as if I could suddenly see what was normally invisible even to me. There was a small layer of energy sparking right next to his skin.

If he had that there, then I had power.

"Don't."

My eyes snapped to his.

We were staring at each other in another challenge.

He didn't get it.

I didn't have any other choice.

I WENT FOR HIS ENERGY.

I was in before he could stop me, and whoa.

Whoa!

I was sucked in, but I was all the way in now, not just partially.

I—it was like I was in another dimension.

There was darkness everywhere.

An echo.

Like I was in a cave.

I smelled water.

I could hear the rush of a waterfall next.

I was at an opening, and I was airborne.

I was flying.

The wind was startling, whipping into me.

I tried screaming, but no sound came out.

I was up and around. I was dipping.

I was soaring.

I was free, but I was terrified at the same time.

A shadow was underneath me, not my own. I was going over the ocean.

We rotated, the shadow and I...and I started struggling.

There were large wings.

They spread out as far as I could see.

I felt a rumbling behind me. Inside me.

Then heat. So much heat.

It was unbearable.

It felt like I was in a volcano.

More rumbling.

It was growing. Building.

Something was happening.

I didn't want what was going to happen, to happen.

No, no, no.

A voracious roar and there was fire everywhere.

The earth was being scorched beneath us. The air around us.

Embers were falling everywhere.

I was in a vacuum.

—I came back to the room.

I looked up.

He had his hand wrapped around my wrist, his eyes blazing. I saw the same embers there and knew that'd been him.

A wave of his fury hit me, actually physically slamming into me, and—I heard a muffled curse—then nothing.

8

OHMYGOD!

I woke and I was moving.

We were moving, and I was lying down as he was sitting across from me.

We were in the back of a vehicle.

I sat up, slowly. My head was still groggy, but I looked around. The windows were tinted and we were moving out of the city.

"Where are we going?"

"To a place."

Nik!

"No. We have to go back." Also, "What happened to you being my only shot to get out of there alive?" I said it with such disdain, I could've been a vamp.

"It's a lot easier to move you when you're unconscious."

He had a good point.

"Seriously. When are we turning around?"

He kept staring at his phone, swiping over the screen. "We're not."

"My frie—"

His head lifted, and his eyes were blazing. "—is a demon. She is surrounded by her kind. Contrary to all the shitty things about demons, they're a dying breed. They don't immediately harm one another. Your friend is young, good-looking, and fertile. Nothing will happen to her."

Gross. Just, so gross.

"Fine. Drop me off and I'll—"

"What is your deal?"

Gah. His eyes were so piercing.

I wished he'd go back to looking at his phone.

Feeling my body heat rise, I shifted uncomfortably on the seat. "What do you mean?"

I crossed my arms over my chest.

That didn't feel right.

"Is tonight not the night that's meant for partying among the youth?"

I laid my arms on my lap.

That wasn't better.

"Huh?" I wasn't following him.

Maybe my arms could go under my legs? I could wedge them just underneath.

"You. Tonight. It's been a long time since I've been to this hemisphere, but Halloween is known as a party night? At least over the last century."

Century?

Power increases with age, so knowing this guy was really old was a whole different level of power when he talked about centuries.

I gulped. "What hemisphere do you usually acquaint?"

There I was, sounding all adult-like, or ancient-like.

Also, score another point for me for using 'acquaint' in a full sentence.

"Why are you spending this night chasing a friend who

doesn't need to be chased?" His eyes narrowed. "What are you distracting yourself from?"

Oh.

Damn.

The frog was back in my throat, and just doubled in size.

Damn.

I had to sit there a bit and blink. I—was that what I was doing?

"What's your name?"

I shot him a look, cocking an eyebrow up. "Now you ask? Aren't we a tad bit late for those formalities?"

Another point for 'formalities.'

His gaze just turned more heated, if that was an option.

"What is your name?"

I waited a beat, though I wasn't sure why. I didn't like being called by my full name, but that was my only hang-up with my name.

"I could find out."

Now I flicked my eyes upwards. "I'm sure you could. Who are you, hmm? Want to know my name, I'd like yours first."

He said almost on the same breath as I ended my sentence, "Kieran Raoul."

Kieran—I choked.

Correction.

I *was* choking.

That name. No way.

I snorted, laughing. "Yeah, right."

He only looked at me.

He was serious.

I jerked forward. "No way!"

Kieran Raoul was a story told to us non-humans. A bedtime book to scare us into behaving and not going out to kill humans. He was as ancient as they came, knowing the origins of the vampire species, even the werewolves. It was whispered that the demon masters came to the surface to pay *him* homage, to give him presents. That the messengers above swept down to meet with him personally.

No one knew what he was, but he wasn't supposed to be real. Or alive.

He was a mythical creature to the mythical creatures.

And I was officially lightheaded again.

My voice was so faint, even to my ears. "Legend says that you rule the Eastern Hemisphere."

"I do."

His tone was so monotone, matter-of-fact.

I—I was freaking.

My pulse skyrocketed.

I was feverish, sweating buckets.

My legs took on the definition of a hyperactive kid with restless leg syndrome on steroids.

I had to get out of there.

He was the Big Bad. Like the OG Big Bad.

He could kill me with a thought, or the blink of an eye.

Panic rose up, swirling around and around in me as I tried again to look for a door within jumping distance, or a window I thought I could break.

Kieran Raoul was a killer, above all else.

We had rules to live by, and if anyone broke one, they were instantly incinerated in his hemisphere. At least that was the story we were told when we were younger. The ruler of our hemisphere was Matron Epux, the most earth-like an angel could get to being an archangel, and they were super powerful. But Kieran was something else entirely. He wasn't rumored to be from evil or saint-like roots.

"You're not joking?" I was whispering at this point. "Are you?"

Holding my gaze, he shook his head.

You cannot escape me, so stop looking for a way out. It's insulting.

My breath left me at the same time. I was, once again, left lightheaded, this time for a completely different reason

I couldn't process this. At all.

How did I get here?

I only meant to think that to myself, not directed at him.

Energists do not come out on dissension nights. I sensed you, and then took you. Coincidences rarely happen. You were there on purpose.

I wasn't.

I could tell he didn't believe me.

I tried again. *I didn't wake up and think, "I bet that super powerful badass that I don't think exists is going to be at Nik's club tonight."* I snorted more to myself than him, and glanced out the window. "Especially on the same day I left my boyfriend after I found him mid-thrust in a girl I know."

I was still looking out the window, not really noticing the passing scenery, but at least looking anywhere but at him.

Instantly, I was back there, going into our apartment and hearing the moans, the groans. The roar right as I opened the door.

"He came as you walked in?"

My heart paused at the same time I whipped my head to his.

He could—*he could see what I was seeing!*

Holy invasion of all invasions!

GET OUT OF MY HEAD, YOU MONSTER ASSHOLE!

He winced, but I felt him withdrawing, and I gotta admit, that was a different sensation too. I wasn't sure if I liked it, or was relieved, or disappointed.

That'd be for pondering later, a lot later, preferably a drunk me later.

"What are you planning for me again?"

His eyebrows lowered. "Why?" He blinked a few times, and I was thinking he needed to get that same visualization out of his head now.

Maybe I should invite him back in? I could go through the entire scene.

And the fork. I didn't think I'd ever forget what I did with the fork.

Well. I threw it. At her vagina, then I had a strong urge to get the fuck out of there.

"What are the chances we could stop at a liquor store?"

He tilted his head forward, then blinked. "You were in dire straits to save your demon best friend, and now you're asking if we can pull over to a liquor store?"

I sighed, slouching down in the vehicle. "I'm resigned to my fate. You're right. Nik's probably going to be fine. It's dissension night, she usually avoids those like the plague, but she's old enough where she's supposed to be paying homage, so I get it. Which brings me back to my original plan for the night: getting drunk. Can we stop at a store?" I thought about it. "Can I owe you too? I didn't bring my wallet with me."

Which goes to show how drunk I was when I first left, *or* how blessed I am that I wouldn't need my wallet getting to a nightclub, inside the club, and also with a free drink. I felt like that was all kinds of points owed me.

I grinned. "I'm in 'dire straits' to get liquored up if that's any consolation."

Another point for using 'dire straits.'

He stared at me for ten more seconds before he released the slightest amount of air. He put his phone in his pocket at the same time as he hit a button overhead. "The nearest liquor store, Leon."

"Yes, sire."

Sire. Jeez.

I had no idea how to use that word in a sentence without sounding lame.

"Is there anything else you'd like? Lobster? A fresh human to feed off their energy?"

"Gross. I don't do that."

He was pulling his phone back out as it was buzzing, and he swiped the screen as he responded, "Of course you do, you're an energy sensor."

"Yeah. I sense energy. I don't eat it."

I felt the air shift in the car. Or the energy.

It was suddenly very, very tense, and I held my breath, noting the changes that came over him. His phone was ignored as his gaze was locked on me. I was pinned in place.

"You don't eat energy?"

"No. That's disgusting and a huge violation. Who am I to take their energy from them?"

"A relief to some, sexual to others."

"Huh?"

I'd heard that wrong. Right?

"Where did you grow up?"

"Here."

"You were not taught the proper way to be an energist?"

I grinned. "No, Sire Big Bad Ass. Apparently, I got no clue how to be an energist, which is what I've been all my life."

So many points for me. I got 'energist' in there, *on top* of sire.

"You cannot be an energist and still be alive if you don't eat energy."

"That's really gross. Can we stop talking about eating and energy? I don't want to eat anyone's energy. That's emotion, and other things, and ew. All sorts of ew going on here."

"You're not human."

He made that sound like it was an accusation. "You're not either."

"Psychics are humans who can feel energy, see energy, see auras. That's what you do, but you are not human. You're telling me you eat like a normal human? Their food and all?"

"Yes. What do you eat?" WAIT! "I don't want to know that. Don't tell me that." *Ohmygod!* "Unless you're going to eat me? Are you going to eat me?!" My voice hitched on a high note at the end.

I winced, hearing it.

We all did things we weren't proud of.

"I'm not planning on eating you."

I sank back in my chair. "That's a relief."

"I have a different use for you."

He opened the door and got out.

I looked. We'd arrived outside of Harry Bahls' Liquors.

9

SIRE BAD ASS

FIVE MINUTES LATER, another whiskey bottle in hand, and I was happy.

I asked if I could put on some music. Sire Bad Ass (more points for me) said yes, and twenty minutes later I was now a whole new level of buzzed. A rap song by BRASAH featuring Koda was filling the air, and the whiskey was barely a burn by now.

"Do you know the language this song is in?"

I shook my head. "Not a clue. It came up as a recommended song on my Spotify." I gave him a tipsy grin. "Do you?"

His eyes darkened. "Yes."

Oh. Well, I wasn't curious enough to ask what the song was about. The title said "Blue Jeans" so I had a good guess what it was about.

"So where are we going now?"

He looked at me, at the whiskey, and I could swear a flash of envy flashed there. Then it was gone, but so was his phone. He stuffed it into his pocket and swiped my booze.

"Hey!" I started to sit up, but he motioned to me.

"Sit down."

I watched as he took a drink, and nothing. The corners of that impossibly pretty mouth of his turned down at the ends. "It's been a century since I've drunk like a normal human. I forgot what something like this tasted like." He handed it back. "I can see why I forgot it."

I glared at him, swiping it and cradling it like it was a baby to my chest. I stroked the neck. "Don't listen to the Big Bad. He's too worldly to appreciate what we lower beings worship."

His head turned to view the outside, but the edge of his mouth lifted. "Maybe. I'm used to power blasting me. Envy. Greed. Hate. Ruthlessness. Deadliness. I wade among the best of the best, the most dangerous in your eyes, and I'm one of them, and yet," he paused, that corner of his mouth curving higher as a wry tone left him, "I find myself enjoying this car ride more than I've enjoyed anything else in the last hundred years." Those very penetrating and probing eyes came to me, and if it were possible, they softened. "You have indeed entertained me."

"It's the rap."

He barked out a laugh, then stopped, his eyes widening.

I had a hunch he couldn't remember the last time he laughed either.

"Can I ask you a question?"

"Sure. Why not?" I knew he was teasing me, but I ignored it.

I asked, "Where are we going? For real."

"For real?" That slightly admonishing tone was back, but his eyes had warmed. "I'm not familiar with that phrase."

"It means be real with me."

"We're going to see someone."

Some of my buzz started to lessen. "That doesn't sound fun."

"Because it won't be, for you."

"What?"

The air was still again.

Though I was a lot more liquored up than I thought I'd be.

I sat up, and the vehicle started to dip a little bit.

A whole lot more.

I was thinking back, remembering.

He was the one who went into the store. I went with him, but he picked up the bottle. He took it to the counter. He paid for it, and he handed it off to the driver. There hadn't been a second's hesitation. He stepped back, motioned for me to walk with him, and we went to the vehicle.

We rounded to my side.

The door was opened.

The driver had been coming around the front of the vehicle, and he handed off the bottle to Kieran.

Kieran passed it to me.

I got in and hadn't thought about it. I just started drinking.

A pair of white butt cheeks in mid-thrust was still on replay in my head. I was laser focused on that bad memory and keen to drink it out of me.

I looked at the bottle. I'd only had a third of it.

I shouldn't be this drunk.

I turned back to him. "You drugged me."

He grinned, and I wasn't too drunk to notice how my entire body lit up at that sight. Damn, but he was really pretty. He shook his head, his tone wry. "It's a spell to put you to sleep. Nothing else. As much as I've enjoyed your commentary and thoughts, I do need to do some work."

"What kind of work?"

"You."

"Me?"

My eyelids were getting a lot heavier.

I was going to fall asleep, but he was talking. I needed more information.

I also needed to come to terms with the fact that I'd been kidnapped.

Why hadn't I tried to run away?

Right.

Because of him.

That'd be useless.

I needed—I needed to stay awake. I was seeing a shimmer of his energy, the one that was tight against his skin, and I couldn't help myself. A little bite, and I'd have enough energy to stay away.

I reached for it, and I took a small strand, the thinnest, and I did what I told him I never did.

I took a bite.

Someone should've warned me about what would happen next.

I WAS PULLED BACK into that same dark place as the last time I touched his energy, but I was held suspended in the air. I felt his breath on the back of my neck, and my body warmed.

Tingles traveled down my spine.

I felt a caress around my throat, then the feel of him behind me.

He fit his body to mine.

A throbbing started inside of me.

I wanted him.

Badly.

Arms encircled me, and he began moving against me. So slowly. So sensually.

I gasped.

Another caress started down my back, and I arched into it, wanting more. Needing more.

I'd never experienced this with anyone else. Just tuning into him, and I was almost panting.

Yearning and wanton desire crawled under my skin, exploring my body, pushing to all my extremities. My legs. My toes. Fingers. Nails.

My heart was pounding.

My vision was blurred.

It was only the touch of him holding me captive.

I would've done anything for him in that moment.

I felt more of his touch rising up my legs, my calves, my knees, my thighs, and a slight pressure.

I was rolled to my back, and my legs parted.

He was above me, and moving over me, and I felt that same touch between my legs.

I wanted him to sheath himself inside of me, thrusting in, all the way in, and then, just like that—I was yanked back, and out.

I was brought back to the vehicle, and Kieran was watching me from across the seat, a shrewd look in his eyes. Cold blasted me, not from the air conditioner, and I began shivering.

I was yearning again, but yearning to go back to what that was. I felt warm and desired.

Was that what he meant about it being sexual for others? HO-LEE-SHIT.

A carnal and primitive desire was lacing through me, and it was as if I'd been awakened. Every cell in my body was crying in protest.

I tasted my tears before I realized I was crying.

As I stared at him, he was merely watching me. That same look in his eyes.

Waiting. He was waiting for something. For me?

But not even a second later, I knew what he was waiting for.

A new hunger was rising in me. I could feel everything in my body. How my foot curved. The ligaments connecting each of my bones. The muscles. The tendons. There was more. My power. It was so deeply entrenched.

He'd been right.

I could feel it now.

And it was starving.

I gaped, only able to open and close my mouth like a fish.

I needed more. Just a little bit more.

I didn't know what, though. More. That was it.

That power was its own creature. It was stirring, stretching. It needed to be fed.

That was me. In me. I had the power to feed its every desire.

He'd been dormant. He? No, she. My power was feminine, and she was hissing. I could feel her moving all my organs, seeking whatever she needed to be fed.

I was moving on the seat without knowing my own body. Writhing around. Curling into a ball, stretching back out, my arms yanking over my head. My toes pointed downwards. My stomach levitated upward.

My back with it, but hunching over in its own stretch.

I felt like I was performing six different yoga poses all at the same time.

"Please," I gasped, my eyes watering as I stared at Kieran.

I didn't know what I was asking for, or why I was asking him, but she had started to take control of me. Not me. Her. I had another whole creature inside of me—from that one forbidden taste of his energy—and she wanted him.

His eyes had darkened by now, molten.

"Please," I rasped again.

"Your kind is only half human, and you've not been feeding your other side. Because of this, there's a separation inside of you. You are almost two beings now. Human and her. You must feed to start merging again."

I didn't know what he was talking about, but I was hungry.

I wanted everything.

His energy. His body. I wanted human food too. Everything and anything. I just needed this feeling to be sated.

"What do I do?"

He continued to watch me, and he didn't respond.

My body began moving toward him, but an invisible wall hit me back. *No* sounded loudly in my head. The voice didn't sound like it came from him, though. It was a low roar, less powerful in its sound but equally as powerful in its determination to be fed.

Please, I said to that voice.

He is above your hunger. That's like waking up as a child and being fed caviar for your first meal.

Caviar isn't even good as a human, buddy. She took over again, growling, whimpering, and my body was flailing on the seat.

I need. Now.

She was back to roaring too.

I was starting to pant and sweat. The need for what she demanded was taking a toll on me. I was becoming blinded by the urgency of feeding the beast that I'd awakened.

"You cannot overcome me."

"I'm not trying to. What do I need here?!"

A strangled cry ripped from my throat.

"You need to eat on energy, which you should've been schooled in when you were born. Your elders did not do their job for you, and now you must pay for the negligence."

"No one eats energy in my family."

"Bullshit. Every energist eats energy. If done properly, you can rid a human of their negative emotions. It can be a mutually beneficial relationship, but it's too late for you to move into that type of relationship. I've never seen an energist so separated from their human form like I see in you. It's fascinating."

She hissed, rearing back, and she shot forward, trying to break through his wall.

NO!

That male roar again, speaking from inside of him this time.

I/she was slammed back, retracting as if I'd been burned.

"Your kind used to be used as sexual servants. They would be starved until they didn't care who they fed on. They could be used for days and days, and if properly handled, they could reach a high that they'd never want to come down from."

This was the warning I always knew could happen to my kind. I'd seen it happen. An uncle who never came home. A cousin who was whisked off by a vampire lord and we never heard from her again.

A shudder went through me, dampening some of the hold my creature had on me.

But she was still whispering in my head, *Please, please, please.* I knew he could hear her. She was speaking to him.

It was working.

He began looking over me, from head to toe, and I felt the same caresses that had happened when I touched his energy. They began again, touching the base of my spine. I gasped, pleasure coursing through me. They touched again, on the inside of my thigh, and I mewled in desire.

That felt so good.

What are you going to do with me?

Give in to me, I added in my head.

A tsking came from him, and it was mocking. *If I give in to you, you will be addicted to me. You'll follow me wherever I may go. The need will be too powerful for you to fight, and you'll eventually die because you would have starved yourself. It would be my energy or no energy, and yes, this has happened to others of your kind. I had two energist lovers two centuries ago. Once I had*

my fill of them, they shriveled up and withered away because they
wouldn't touch another unless it was me.

My word. Ego, much?

He continued to watch me, but I felt his surprise, and his
amusement. Even that seemed to surprise him.

"I've never had one of you be this starved and give me sass at
the same time. Perhaps your human is strong inside of you."

I stopped listening to him.

I needed to get back in control.

Images of him letting me loose on someone I didn't want to be
with horrified me.

I knew where this would go. I'd start eating their energy, but it
would turn sexual and there was no one I wanted to be intimate with.
Not like this. That would haunt me if he turned me on someone else...
yet eating solely on his energy sounded completely out of the picture.

Though, I still wanted to, and just the thought was making
me ache for him, but I was blaming those raging hormones on
what he said. A starved creature was inside of me.

I couldn't believe this was happening to me.

I'd never been helpless to my monster.

It was something I prided myself on.

Nikki had been at times. She gave into her demon and there'd
been a few nights when we had to do something that we'd been
ashamed about. It's what happened when you were one of us.
There were slip ups.

Except me. I never slipped up, but watching him, panting for
him, feeling those same caresses from him all over my body, I
could see it happening. My power wanted his power. That's what
was going on. She was begging for it, and he was starting to give
in. I could feel the weakening inside of him.

I was in there, inside of him. That realization hit me.

It shocked me.

No one's been in your head, have they?

His eyelids started to drop, but at my voice, his gaze shot back to mine. I saw his alarm, but I also felt it too.

I was right. I was in there, and no one had been in there.

You are indeed more powerful than I thought.

Please, a whispered plea in my head. It came from deep within me, but again, I didn't know what I was asking for. It felt stronger, more focused, more important. It wasn't sexual and it wasn't hungry. There was more happening here, and none of it was making sense to me.

So many emotions and vibrations were swimming around us in the back of his vehicle.

A break inside of him. A small crack, and I felt some of his resistance crumble.

I slipped inside, and he was there, waiting for me.

He wrapped me up, holding me in the air.

Our bodies were across from each other in his vehicle. I was still on my side, and he was frozen on his end, but our creatures were meeting each other in the unseen. I wasn't in his head, but I was inside of him. Somehow.

He was staring at me, his eyes dark with sensual promises as he enveloped me.

He closed his eyes. So did I, and we were both in our creatures.

His power was a strong beat of a drum, echoing around us and filling us both.

This was what I had been asking for, to be sated by his power.

All I had to do was be there, and I was basking in it. We both were, but his head lifted. His gaze found me. An awareness settled between us, pulling us both to each other as if we were on opposite ends of a rope.

We came together, and as his power kept beating around us, spreading out in echoed ripples, he lowered his mouth to my neck. I moved my head aside, giving him better access, and his tongue touched my skin. A taste. I jumped from the sensations.

Another lingering taste.

My body leaned into his.

He was holding me to him.

His hands splaying down over my hips, keeping me anchored in place, and he continued tasting my throat.

A low rumble began from inside of him.

Its sound came from deep in the earth, from beneath us. I felt the ground move from the sound of it, and I knew that was his beast. He was waking.

My hands came to his chest, my fingers splayed out. His heartbeat was there, in perfect rhythm from the beat spreading around us.

That rumbling sensation from beneath us grew stronger, more insistent.

His mouth moved more insistently over me, moving to the base of my neck and he explored down. Down. Between my breasts.

I arched backwards, my head falling back. I was almost help-less to his hold. He could've done anything to me, and I would've ached for more. Always more.

He tilted me in his arms, moving me to the side as one of his hands found my center and I gasped as he moved inside of me, filling me.

My throbbing ache began its own drumbeat of sound. His. Mine, but smaller.

His. Mine, but smaller.

He moved inside of me, thrusting in the same staccato as our beats, and all the while the ground kept moving.

I felt that beast moving under the surface, moving. Gliding. It was looking for an opening, and he was going to rise.

Kieran clamped down on a growl, his arms holding me tight,

as he dug deeper into me and he moved faster, at a more insistent pace. His mouth moved back up my chest, my throat, my jawline, over my cheek, to my ear, and he breathed there.

"Come for me."

It was a guttural command in my ear, and I gritted my teeth, holding on as the sensations were building higher and higher.

Another impatient growl from him as the earth's shaking became more and more, almost nonstop. He bit out a curse word before moving, and his mouth clamped down on me, his fingers moving inside of me still.

I exploded, hurdling over the edge, and my entire body came undone in his arms.

He was panting over me, but the earth's surface was still. The beast was settling back down.

He hadn't wanted him to rise up. The power of that feat alone was mind-numbing.

Slowly, and reluctantly, our creature's energies separated.

She was filled so she settled back inside of me, and that's when I opened my eyes, seeing him staring at me with such carnal need that I started to rise. I was going to go over to him.

"Don't!"

His eyes burned at me.

He needed a release, I could feel it from him.

"Don't touch me."

Well, then.

I didn't touch him.

10

QUESADILLA

"I CAN FEEL HER."

I could only handle two minutes of silence. It felt like twenty.

Kieran expelled a ragged and annoyed-sounding breath of air. "Are you shitting me?"

I peered at him, almost squinting. "That's very progressive of you, Mr. Dire Straits and I Speak Like I'm Centuries Old Sire."

He snorted. "I am centuries old. You're a child to me."

"Please." My stomach rolled over. "You'll only cheapen our relationship with that mindset."

A curse from him, and he raked a hand through his hair. "We don't have a relationship."

"You woke my creature. We'll always have a relationship."

There was a beep, and he raised his hand to touch a button. As he did, I caught his slight grin. It was small, but there. And why that made me feel good, I didn't know. I didn't want to know. "Yes?"

The driver said through the intercom, "We've arrived."

"Thank you."

"Where are we?" The vehicle was slowing, turning onto a

rough driveway. I could see gates opening, then we were going through and past tall pillars. There were vampires—well, not actual vampires, but marble ones—guarding the gate, and all of them watched our vehicle pull past them.

"We're here to see someone."

I was suddenly remembering that I was kidnapped, and that he said he had 'plans' for me. The history of my kind was flashing through my mind.

"I think I'm good in the car. You go and have your visit. I'll stay put."

"We're in a vampire compound. You've awakened her, and they'll smell her. A vehicle won't stop them from coming in here, and I'd rather not have to declare war on an entire species. You're coming with me."

The vehicle had stopped, and his door opened.

He waited.

I glanced out my door. A vampire was there, waiting to open it for me.

I moved across my seat. "I think I'm good going inside with you."

He made no sound, but I could feel his amusement as he got out first.

I was second, and he had stepped aside, waiting for me.

The driver was standing outside the door, and as we moved ahead, he shut the door behind us.

It was dark outside, but with my new inner creature, I was seeing in the dark as if it were light. The house in front of us looked like a place that'd be in a horror film, though. Vampires were all around us. On the front porch area, standing around the pillars built into the house. Behind us. I glanced around, and they were even on the gate and a wall that surrounded the compound.

Glancing up, Kieran had been watching me.

He did not seem disturbed at all.

Me? I was perturbed. I stayed away from vampires as a general rule. They tended to like my carotid artery a bit too much for me. I could feel their energy, and it never sat right with me.

I mean, I stayed away from most supernatural beings, with a few exceptions like Nikki, whose demonic side was unnaturally happy, except for nights like tonight. Dissension night. And family members like Ralph, because he got it. He understood.

We always felt like prey.

As a whole, we weren't really aggressive either, which evolution-wise didn't help us.

A grand black door opened, and we went inside.

A vampire fell in step in front of us, and Kieran followed.

It was an old house, with a ballroom on one side and a room with a fireplace on the other. A grand stairwell wrapped up in front of us. We bypassed pretty much everything, going to the back of the house, which seemed to take forever because I was clocking forty vampires that we passed. They were looking down at us from the second floor, and staring at us as we went past, then coming out to congregate in the hallway.

Creepy as fuck.

The room we were shown into looked like a large hall that had more pillars holding up the ceiling. A podium with three large stairs was at the back of the room, complete with a throne. The chair was big enough to sit four people, and the back of it almost touched the ceiling.

A lone body lounged on the chair. *Gee, overkill much?*

I couldn't tell if he or she was a female or male. He had feminine features, so her face looked soft, but the energy was masculine. They rose, and as their eyes saw me, they lit up. "You've brought me a gift, Kieran."

She had a soft, feminine tone, and she clapped her hands together. "I'm so excited. And it's a newly born energist. Even better."

Kieran didn't spare me a look. "For you? I thought she'd been sent from you. I found her in my nightclub."

She paused, her head cocking to the side. "Right. You own the new demon bar, Bass. Such a trite establishment. I don't know why you'd want to own that building."

"Right. Because you wouldn't want to own the opening for where the demon masters submerge? I have a hard time believing that." He stepped aside and nodded to me. "She came to me in the oddest chain of events, and since at the heart of it was one of yours, I was sure she was a present from you."

What?

The vampiress still didn't move. She seemed almost like a statue, and she touched her chest with a dainty hand. "Please, Kieran. I'm riveted. Tell me more." As she spoke, she turned her hand, and one of her nails cut her own skin. She drew a line down between her breasts, leaning back in her chair. Blood began to pool out, and with a flick of a wrist, she was descended upon by three other vampires. All who sucked from that trail of blood, and as they sank their teeth into her, she gasped, grasping the back of one of the vampires' heads.

The sexual and hunger-filled energy rolled off all of them, and as the first wave of her energy rolled over me, her eyes were studying my every reaction.

She did that on purpose.

I had to steel myself against how my own creature started stirring, awakening again, but *she* only wanted Kieran.

He was right. One taste and she wouldn't be sated with anyone else. This was going to be a dilemma, *indeed.*

She's testing you, seeing how I react to you. Quell your beast.

What's her name on the throne?

Quessadiline.

Quesadilla just climaxed up there.

The ripples of it left her body, but a fourth vampire joined the tasting, and as he did, he moved to crawl up her body. She leaned farther back, holding the back of his head now as he positioned himself between her legs.

"Should we give you a moment?" Kieran's voice almost sounded bored. "Or should I take this as an insult to my visit?"

The fourth vampire thrust inside of her at his second statement, but as fast as that happened, the four vampires were thrown away from her. She pulled at her clothes to cover her and sat up. "I do apologize. I couldn't help myself. A little fun with your new pet, Kieran." She fluffed her hair and relaxed back. "Now...tell me how you feel she was a gift sent by myself when I insist she's a present given from you."

"Your vampire seduced her boyfriend."

Wait. What?!

He kept on, "And she did this at a time when this energist would find them."

Is this true? I asked him.

He ignored me, his jaw tightening. "And she was given persuasion by your vampire to pack her things, to leave her boyfriend, and to go and see her best friend, whom you insured was working at my nightclub tonight. On a night you knew I'd be there. So, yes, Quessadiline, I do fully believe that this energist was a gift from you."

"Why would I send you an energist? They're like toys to us."

"They're also used as weapons of distraction, and you knew I had kept two others with me centuries ago."

My knees gave out at the reminder of how old Kieran was.

"You were hoping to distract me tonight because I know that while I took the time to travel to see you, you sent thirty vampires to attack Bass tonight."

A hard glint appeared in her eyes, and Kieran was right.

I saw it. The satisfaction that rolled off of her was pure evil.

She smiled slowly as she preened. "Why would I do that tonight? Of all nights?"

"Because you knew four of the six masters would be above earth today, and it was your first move against taking charge of the underworld."

Kieran was calm. I pricked at the inside of his head, and he shoved me out. Okay. Maybe he wasn't totally calm, but he was giving that impression...at least his energy was all calm.

Quessadiline stood up from her throne, and she stepped to the edge of the podium.

A cruel smile teased over her face. "Maybe I have done all of that, but you said thirty before, Kieran." A pause. "Try three hundred."

A wave of smug and sick triumph flared around the entire room, and I could feel others' emotions join in from the hallway. They were all listening to us. I didn't know how. I didn't know much about vampires on purpose, but I wouldn't have been surprised if there wasn't a telepathic connection between them all.

She threw her card down.

"No, Quessadiline. I said thirty because that's how many I left alive."

Kieran just swept the whole deck.

11

SHE/I

A SNARL ERUPTED from Quessadiline before she attacked.

After that, it was pandemonium.

I had no idea what was going on, but it was all happening at the same time.

Kieran met Quesadilla, as vampires from around the room launched at me.

Not aggressive: me.

Them: very aggressive.

I noticed more vampires streaming in from the hallway, but I was snatched backwards and looked up. Kieran had a hold on me.

Fight!

I don't know how. I mean, I threw a fork at the vamp bitch who seduced my ex.

Let your creature loose.

How?!

I had no clue how he was holding Quesadilla off, but she looked frozen in mid-air. It was remarkable, and he was doing the same with the other vampires. No one could get to us, but whatever hold he had on them wasn't going to last. They were breaking through, inch by inch. That much I could feel. And everyone here was immortal...but I wasn't.

I couldn't stay here for the rest of my life.

Use your energy. Take theirs.

Eat them? I was revolted.

No. You don't have to eat everything.

There was a joke there, but I was refraining.

He kept on. *You can literally take their energy.*

I can?

You are so severely unschooled. How are you still alive?

You have a right to be frustrated, but I didn't choose to walk into Vampire Quesadilla's campus. You brought me here knowing what I wasn't capable of.

A guttural growl was coming from him.

No.

I looked down.

That wasn't a growl, that was the floor shaking.

I glanced outside. The wall was starting to crumble, and the trees were shaking violently.

Nope. Not the floor. The earth was shaking.

Seriously, who was this guy? I knew it was his creature rising, and here I was thinking there was no creature I knew that could rise like his could. A lot of beings were underground, but none that I knew that had a body above the surface.

Whoa!

I yelled in my head, my entire body jerking.

Stop. He was in my head, and he was speaking to my creature. *She's clueless. You need to wake and hel—*

HOLY FUCKING HELL!

She rose and she rose fast.

She hurled herself from wherever I'd been storing her, and after that, I held on as things happened, things I did, things that I knew I'd never forget.

I rose in the air, or she rose in the air, and as if I was watching myself from outside of my body, she shot her hand out. A command sparked from her eyes, and she pulled the energy from every single vampire in the room. Not just the room. Energy was streaming in from the hallways, and a back door was thrown open. More energy burst from it.

As I watched, as she took the energy and seemed to harness it around us, the vampires dropped to the ground.

They had no energy left. The more they exerted, she took it, and she was using it to fuel herself/us and Kieran. Because of it, the ground stopped shaking, and whatever creature he had inside wasn't rising any longer.

He inhaled the energy, and I watched as it went through his body.

He leapt, a sword materializing in his hand as he did, and he made one motion with it. He completed the motion at the same time that he dropped to the ground.

A second later, he waited, stepping back toward us/her.

She/I was still draining the energy from the vampires, but we watched as Quesadilla's head slowly fell off her body.

Before our eyes, she crumbled to the ground. The rest of her vampires crumbled as well. I felt all of their hearts stop...and I was waiting.

I glanced at Kieran. "No dust?"

A flare of annoyance flashed over his face, just as the sword vanished from his hand. "This is not a fucking television show."

"Oh."

My voice sounded weird. It was a mix of hers and mine. Hearing her voice now, and not in my head, was surreal. As fast as she rose, she returned back to where I kept her, and she was purring like a cat now.

"I thought you said I didn't need to eat their energy."

He was walking across the room for a phone that had

dropped from Quesadilla's body. He spared me a look as he bent for it. "You didn't eat their energy, but you used it to fight them. Your creature will be sated for five years on what they gave her tonight."

Oh. Good to know. I guess.

"How'd you know all that stuff, about the vamp who seduced my ex?"

"I didn't. I was reading her mind."

Oh.

Wait.

"She sent three-hundred vamps to that club."

He gave me a grim look. "She did."

"Would they die like these did when you killed her?"

He was going through her phone but looked up at me. "I didn't kill her."

I looked at the head that had rolled from her body. "How more dead do they have to be?"

"Her body and head will need to be burned, as well as all of the vampires here. She might be dead. She's connected to them. If one lives, she can survive off that one vampire until a new body's been made for her."

"What?"

Holy crap.

"They're like the scourge of the Earth. How do you know— never mind. I don't want to know. I'll get depressed from the answer, no matter what it is." As I was talking to myself, he used his phone to make a call.

They answered, and he said, "I need Quessadiline's entire compound burned."

"You got her?"

"I got her."

"Got it."

He hung up and made another call as he started to leave the room.

I hurried after him, and I was running since he was moving so fast.

The front door was opened and we stepped out, the vehicle still there and his driver waiting.

The second call answered and Kieran said as he got inside, "You have three-hundred vampires heading to Bass. We'll be too late."

I was moving around to my door when his words hit me.

I had known. He said it inside, but my knees locked when it registered.

Nik.

Nik was at Bass.

Three-hundred vampires against those demons? Demons didn't have 'connections' to keep each other alive like vampires did. And I knew demons better. They'd hiss and fight. They had superhuman strength at times. Some could use magic, but most couldn't. It was something the masters kept to themselves, so no one rose to challenge them.

Nik was going to die.

Once our vehicle was on the way, I turned to him. "My best friend is at stake. I don't give a fuck what you are, but whatever you are, unleash him. Now."

We were speeding away.

He turned to lock eyes with me, and after we traveled a little farther, vehicles sped past us. They slowed, turning into the compound.

I had a feeling we'd be seeing flames soon too.

I didn't care.

I only cared about Nikki.

"What are you?"

"I'm a dragon."

12

HARRY BAHLS'

THERE WERE stories and movies galore about dragons, but in the real supernatural world, they didn't exist. No. That wasn't true. Two were known to have existed, and they were almost as old as the Earth. Almost.

It was rumored that a fight broke out among the two dragons, and that's how the seven continents were formed, from their fighting. It was also known that one dragon won, killing the other, and now the dots were connecting because that dragon was rumored to exist in the Eastern Hemisphere.

It made sense.

It was how he could do what he did against Quesadilla, because killing a vampiress was nothing to sneeze at. But he did it, granted, he had some help from me, but it was almost a joke because he could've killed everyone in that compound without my help.

He was watching, waiting for my reaction.

"Why did you use me back there? You could've killed all of them without me raising a finger." And without the perceived threat of his creature rising.

Why?

Humiliation sliced through my chest.

"Because you need to play catch-up on your training."

He wasn't even lying about his lying.

"And now?" I was trying not to sound bitter here, but I was.

"You can be at Bass in no time. My friend can teleport five feet. A dragon is so much more powerful than any demon master."

"Yes. I could, but I won't."

"Why?" I cried out. "She's my best friend."

"And she'll survive. They'll all survive."

"Oh. Well, thank you."

"Don't thank me."

I just eyed him. Wariness was overtaking me.

He added, "You're going to kill the vampires for me."

"What?"

"I have colleagues who are holding everyone for us. They started their attack. I was too late in reading Quessadiline's mind to make a call, but people I know got there in time before too many were killed. The demon masters have already gone back underground."

"Of course," I bit out. *Typical demon.*

––––––––––

THE DRIVE BACK TOOK FOREVER.

Or maybe it was because I knew I'd have to do what I'd done back at the compound, and this time, I knew the stakes. Or the lack of stakes.

Why he was doing this, I didn't know. I didn't ask. I was sure it had to do with 'his plans' for me, but I remained mad the whole drive back.

Or, I tried.

This was me.

I thought my best friend was going to die, then I found out she wasn't, and she so wasn't because a fucking dragon lord didn't want the demons to die. He could snap his fingers and probably all the vampires would be burned where they stood, but no.

My training.

I had to kill the vampires instead.

But yeah, back to me, because not only was I not an aggressive person, I also didn't—couldn't—stay mad. I lacked the energy, which the irony was not lost on me. It was how I was built. It's why I wanted to get drunk tonight and why I threw a fork at the vampire seducer bitch. Even picking up that fork and hurling it at her vagina, I felt bad about it.

I should've thrown harder. And not felt bad as I did it.

But yeah. That was me. The same me who reached between two cushions and pulled out the whiskey bottle from where I stuffed it.

"It's been spelled."

I stuck my tongue out at him, took that cap off, and guzzled as much of the beverage as I could.

The bottle was ripped from me, and his hand was around my throat. He wasn't saying anything, but I felt a burning spreading from him to me. He was evaporating the spell as it trickled down my throat.

It moved slower than the liquid. Good to know for the future.

Once he got the last of the spell, he opened his window and tossed the whiskey out of it.

Damn. I'd been hoping to get drunk at least. I was due. This was a truly shitty Halloween.

"Can I get some music turned on?"

"No."

Okay, then.

"So, you're a dragon. How does that work again? Is it true that dragons live in a flipside alternate universe or something? And you're the only one who merges with one of them?"

I was acting like I knew. I was bullshitting, but those were the rumors I heard. Our kind of ghost stories, or I thought so before I met him.

He grinned. "Let's keep it a mystery, hmm?" He went back to his phone.

For an old dude, he was with the times being on the phone so much. I was tempted to throw his phone out like he threw out my whiskey. Then I remembered he's a dragon and there's no reason for him not to kill me.

Which made me wonder... "Why am I alive?"

"What?"

"You found out I was supposed to be a distraction." I was now thinking about that, if that had actually happened how Quesadilla wanted. I would've been sexed up, and then what? Tossed out as Nikki would've been killed? "Quesadilla did all that so she could make a move on the underground? I didn't know you guys were so ambitious."

"Everyone wants more power, and you're talking as if you're not one of us."

"Right. So why haven't you killed me yet?"

"I'm asking myself the same question right now."

He said that under his breath, and he paused a moment, blinked, then went back to the phone.

"How'd you find all that out about my ex?"

He gave me a look.

"Right. You read her mind. I know you can read mine, so does that mean you can read all minds?"

"Yes."

"Whoa." I thought about that. "Is that annoying? Or handy? Or—" I looked over.

He was glaring at me.

"Right." I grinned and pointed to my head. "I can just think my questions to you, which is probably for the best because I have a lot."

"I am not telling you about my dragon."

"I'm noting that you didn't say 'me' when you're referring to your dragon. So it's like my creature and me?"

No. It's not the same—

I felt a full blast of energy at me, which would've made me happy. Right now, not so much. He forced me out of his head. Or were we in my head? I was losing track. There was so much new information happening, and to think, when I started my trek tonight, I just thought I could convince Nikki to go back to her apartment with me and get drunk. Maybe we'd dress up as ourselves and go trick-or-treating. Some old people were happy anyone rang their doorbell for treats. They didn't care how old we were, or if our breaths matched the smell of their mouth wash.

"I should've listened to Ralph."

"Who's Ralph?"

"My cousin. He told me not to go to Bass tonight." I side-eyed him. "You wouldn't have met me. How much better would your night have been?"

He raised an eyebrow. "You're right. I would've just killed all the vampires myself, then tracked down Quessadiline who would've gone on the run."

"Right."

He was eyeing me back, with the hint of a faint smile. "I could've been at Quessadiline's in an instant, and I could be back at Bass just as fast. Maybe think on that?"

I did, and...me! It was me.

I was the reason.

What did that mean?

Stop. Just stop.

Stopping.

A break.

Can we stop at Harry Bahls' again?

Yes, please. I need liquor at this point, too.

See. I loved how I could grow on a dragon.

13

ANTI-CLIMACTIC

It was almost anti-climactic when we got back to Bass.

I knew what he wanted this time, and we walked inside. I saw that when he said he had 'people' holding everything for me, he meant witches. There were four of them in the building and they were chanting their spells.

Witches and I don't get along either.

They always instantly know who I am, and are paranoid I'm going to take their energy.

I used to think they were crazy, but now I know what I can actually do and note to self, I may do just that to torture them in the future.

Again: witches and I don't get along.

Three of the four glared at me. The fourth didn't. She must've been the 'me' of the group because she gave me a bright smile. She didn't look altogether, if you get my drift. But back to the business at hand.

Kieran said everything was on hold...and he really meant it. The vampires and demons were frozen in mid-battle. I had to make sure Nikki was safe, so I did a scan, and spotting her on the second floor, I went over. Taking her hand, I dragged her after me. She was still 'frozen,' so it was a weird sensation, but I gave Kieran a look.

I'll be back. You can wait a few more minutes.

Nadeem.

It was the first time he said my last name, and looking back, I thought, *Since when did you take the time to learn my name?*

He raised an eyebrow back at me. *Micaela Nadeem. You were born to Avi and Henrietta Nadeem. You have three sisters and four brothers. You have eighteen cousins in the Twin Cities' area. Thirty relatives total here. You're best friends to Nikki Atkinson, who is sleeping with—*

Okay, okay. My night's not too bad. Don't destroy it completely by saying his name.

I faked a shudder but grabbed for Nikki's phone and called Ralph.

He pulled up ten minutes later, and I seat-belted her in.

"Wha— Is she going to be like that the whole time? I don't do personal arrivals, Ca—"

"You will this time, because if you don't, I'll tell your mother you smoke pot when you're working."

He opened his mouth and glowered at me. "Not cool, Caley Girl. Not freaking cool."

I gave him a pointed look back, but he pulled away and I felt a weight off my shoulder.

Mission complete. My best friend was safe.

I was silently hoping the unfreeze would wear off? I hadn't thought that through.

I went back inside, took my position by Kieran, and dipped my head.

"Ready to unleash the creature, Draco."

He growled in my head. *Do not call me that name.*

I grinned, and the witches let chaos reconvene.

14

MY BUSINESS

KIERAN'S DRIVER dropped me off outside Nikki's place, and it'd been egged.

Nice. Lovely.

The words, 'No candy! U Sux,' were spray painted across the front. As I was getting out of the vehicle, the door opened and Nikki came out, a coffee in hand. She pointed to the graffiti over her shoulder as she came down the stairs toward me. "Your cousin sucks too. I was still frozen, and he put me on the front steps facing my place. I enjoyed a full hour of watching the graffiti glow in the dark before daylight hit and I unfroze." She handed over the coffee. "I was actually sleeping most of the night so I'm rested. My phone's been blaring since I got unstuck. You, on the other hand, look like you need this."

Pumpkin spice.

I loved my girl.

She grinned. "Three shots of espresso."

I groaned. "I love you, I love you, I love you."

I was too exhausted to go anywhere else, so I sat. She sat beside me.

We stared at the street as a couple candy wrappers drifted past us.

"Thank you for coming and trying to save me."

I needed some pumpkin first. "I did save you. I got you in Ralph's Uber."

She grinned. "I know, but I heard the story. Heard what you did."

What I did.

I had to let that process for a bit because I'd been there and I wasn't sure I believed it myself.

"I guess there's a creature inside of me that needs to eat energy."

"I hear ya. My demon really likes raw steak, but I'm vegan. Talk about a filibuster."

I frowned. "That's not what that word means."

She shrugged. "It should. It sounds accurate."

"Pretty sure it has to do with politics."

She snorted. "That's funny."

"Did you get to see your master?"

She shook her head. "No. The vamps got there before I was up in line, then the coven came in and it was a long couple hours of just waiting. They don't tell you that when you're frozen, your bladder doesn't freeze."

"Oh."

"Let's not talk about that."

"Okay."

She looked over again, her face softening. "I'm sorry about you and Jay."

Right. The catalyst of the entire night.

I shrugged this time. "The relationship had been done for a while, so I'm not too surprised. But it did turn out that he'd been seduced by a vamp and she used some persuasion magic on sending me to you."

Another snort. "I don't buy it. You would've left him anyways. It was due time. And I doubt Jay needed much seducing. He's been getting with other vamps for a while."

I looked at her, eyebrows raised. "This is something a best friend should've relayed to me. What the hell?"

"You really liked him in high school, and the relationship *has* been done. Everyone knew, but you were still denying it. I'm not going to be the messenger."

"Nikki!"

"What? I'm a demon. I'm not perfect. Also, it's not like I didn't have your back. Every girl that hooked up with him got barred from Bass. Why do you think some of the guys from work don't like you? When I say everyone's been waiting for this breakup, literally everyone has been waiting." She flashed a wide smile. "But chin up, word is that the new boss got his hooks in you. Tell me about him." She was wiggling her eyebrows up and down.

"You haven't met him?"

She shook her head, her smile lessening a notch. "He's just as much of a mystery to us too. We heard he was there last night. I guess the masters wanted to speak to him, but everything happened and you know what happened. There's a staff meeting later today so maybe he'll be there."

He wouldn't.

I knew this because I felt his absence, and I could feel it because there was a hollow ache smack in the middle of my chest.

After I helped with the vampires, Kieran had been watching me the whole time. I'd been so tuned into him, so aware of him, that it had made my concentration difficult. He knew it too, and then his creature's spirit joined mine and everything went erotic and violent at the same time. When his creature's spirit merged with mine, I could feel everything about Kieran. I could taste him. I could touch him. I was him.

I mean, I knew I wasn't.

It was his dragon's spirit, but the rush of power was next level. Literally.

The vampires were sucked dry by both of us, and when a fire was started, Kieran ushered me outside right away. I was bundled into his vehicle, and his driver took off. I watched Kieran the whole time, feeling his dragon still with me, but a block away from Nikki's apartment, I also felt Kieran call his dragon back to him.

He hadn't wanted to go. He did it, reluctantly and slowly, and it felt like he'd been peeled off me. It hurt, both of us. I could feel his pain, and I was feeling his loss now too.

No, returning to what Nikki just said.

Kieran wouldn't be there. He was already gone.

I didn't know why he bought Bass, what he was doing in our hemisphere, and I tried telling myself that it was none of my business.

The only problem after Nikki and I went back inside, after I tried curling up in bed for a nap, and even later into the week was that I couldn't shake the feeling that it was my business.

I just wasn't sure why.

15

RAKON

TWO WEEKS LATER.

"Hey."

I jerked upright in bed.

It was dark out, and I glanced at the clock. Three in the morning.

My pulse was fast, and I was sweating a little.

A breeze came in through the open window. Looking over, a street light was shining right into my bedroom. Well, Nikki's guest bedroom, but it was mine since it looked like I was her roommate for a bit.

Hey.

I jerked again. That voice was...

Kieran?

No. Well. Yes. Kinda.

It was a deep voice and growling, but not growling at the same time.

My heart started to pound harder, more insistent.

Thud.

Thud.

Thud.

It was Kieran's dragon.

Is Kieran okay? Is he hurt?

Why did I care so much?

He's fine. He's busy right now.

So busy he wouldn't know his dragon was reaching out?

What's he doing?

He's busy.

Busy?

Busy.

Understanding flooded me.

He was having sex.

I wanted to growl, but damn. My body got heated, and why was I caring about that either?

He was hot, rich, super freaking powerful so of course he could get some. Easy.

Not caring.

Nope.

That wasn't me.

We were now a few weeks past Halloween, and my creature was getting restless. Hungry. She was missing Kieran. She was. Not me. Nada.

I rolled my eyes at myself. One would think the breakup had been with Kieran and not a guy who I'd been with for four years.

Are you okay?

I am.

He sounded good. Happy.

Why are you reaching out?

I missed you guys.

Guys? Me and—

Her. She's my mate.

Shock seized me for a second.

Mate.

He said that, right?

She's your what?

My creature didn't speak. At least, not that I knew of, but I felt her. She was moving in me, wanting to take over, and I knew what she wanted. She wanted to have creature spirit sex with Kieran's dragon.

My mate. It's why Kieran was compelled to help you that night. I've been missing you and he won't listen to me.

She was railing inside of me, wanting, needing to get out. I was struggling to keep her in, especially because I've not been eating—

You've not been eating?

I froze again. That wasn't his dragon anymore.

Kieran?

You've not been eating?

Funny. He sounded a lot like his dragon with that growl.

I've been eating.

I heard him growl from his end. *Energy, Micaela. Have you been eating energy?*

I wasn't swooning at hearing him say my name.

I normally hated hearing people say my full name, and I wasn't swooning when he said it. I wasn't light-headed. Not one bit.

I sighed, melting back down onto my pillow and I curled up into the blankets.

I was swooning. I needed to energist-up and admit it.

Yes. Got it. Swoon. Get your shit together. You haven't been eating?

I forgot he could read my thoughts.

Micaela!

It's CALE, dude!

I could hear his growl in my head. Nope. Correction: I could feel his growl, it was echoing through my body.

I wasn't so swoony anymore.

Micaela, you need to eat energy.

I'm fine.

Micaela—

I said I'm fine.

You woke her—

No, you woke her. I didn't do that. You did. She'll go right back—

No. She won't. Not with the level that you woke her up. You were with my dragon. She was with my dragon, and you raised her strength level by taking five hundred vampires.

Five hundred?

There were two hundred vampires at Quessadiline's compound.

If I'd been sitting upright, I would've fallen back. I was floored at that.

Two hundred?

Yes.

You went from amateur hour to the pros in one night. If you haven't been eating energy, you are a danger to people you love.

Oh, come on.

I'm not joking with you. You need to eat now.

I rubbed at my forehead. I'd been sleeping just fine—

You're lying to yourself. You're lying to me. You're lying to both our creatures. Stop insulting everyone's intelligence here.

He said I'm his mate.

Kieran was silent on his end.

Knock, knock.

A growl. *Don't be funny.*

I'm not. He said we're mates.

We're not mates.

I waited.

He was silent. Again.

Kieran!

I could hear his sigh from his end. *Yes, he's told me the same.*

Mates. As in—

I'm aware of what a mate is.

Mates weren't husband and wife. They were soulmates, as in till the end of time type of stuff. As in there was a situation where if we shared blood during sex, and if the M word was involved, we'd be linked—everything stopped.

Kieran.

Another sigh. *What?*

Can you speak like this to others?

He was quiet for a bit. *Yes.*

Relief went through me. My eyes started watering.

But not to the same degree.

That was his dragon.

I could almost feel Kieran shutting up his dragon.

What's he mean by that?

Nothing.

Kieran.

What?

What'd he mean by that?

There was an exchange of growls happening. And I was now noticing that we all enjoyed growling. Interesting.

A fatigue started rising up in my body.

It's the response to your adrenaline. Rakon shouldn't have woken you.

Rakon?

That's his name.

Whoa. Do I need to name my creature?

No, Micaela. Your energy will blend with you eventually so the two of you are merged as one. It's not healthy to be as separated as you are. It's a different situation with Rakon and myself. We're the same, but we're also two separate creatures as well.

Cool. That's all I could think. I knew I should have more of an intelligent response, but the fatigue was rising and rising. A yawn left me. A second one came right on its heel.

You need to sleep, and you need to eat.

I nestled into my pillow, my whole body feeling like it was melting. *Night, Rakon.*

Night, Micaela.

I could feel his wish to merge with my creature, and she stirred. A blast of exhaustion came right after.

You're doing this to me, aren't you?

Kieran didn't respond to that. He said softly in my head, "You need to eat tomorrow."

Yeah...

I was asleep.

16

FUCKING BRAD

A WEEK LATER.

"Since our Halloween sucked, I think we should have a re-do."

Nikki announced that when I got back from classes, and as she was teleporting back and forth from her kitchen to her bedroom. She was getting dressed for a shift at Bass again.

"What?"

She teleported to the bedroom.

Came back, her leather corset outfit on. "I know you don't like Brad, but hear me out."

I growled.

I'd been more forthcoming with them since I noted how Rakon and Kieran liked to do the same.

"Hold on." Poof. She was gone.

"So as I was saying." She was back, braiding her hair in her usual work-style. "You've not said much about Jay, but we were supposed to get drunk that night." Poof, gone. Poof, she was back and she was spraying some red glitter into her hair. "If it hadn't been Dissension Night, we would've done that. And Brad's on this thing where he's wondering if we should try at a relationship or not. I say no, but he's got something up his butt about it. He's having a small gathering tonight. After my shift, we could go over and check it out? What do you think?"

"I have school tomorrow."

She gave me a knowing look, though there was a flash of concern there too. "You and I both know you won't be sleeping. You haven't been since..."

Yeah. Since Halloween, except for the night when Kieran used his power on me.

I changed the subject. Nikki hadn't pushed, but she knew I wasn't sharing something.

"Sure. Why not. Fucking Brad, huh?"

She grimaced. "I mean, I'm the one fucking Brad."

That got a laugh from me. "You know what I mean."

"I do." There was that concern again. It was all front and center, and she crossed the room to stand in front of me. "If you need to talk, I'm here. You know that, right?"

"I do." I smiled, feeling it, because she was there for me. "You should've told me Jay was cheating on me, and you know it."

"I know, but that's not why you were with him, you know."

I looked up, frowning. "What do you mean?"

"You hide from so much. I know your kind does that, but you spent five out of seven nights here anyways. It's why you only had to grab a third of your possessions. The rest was already here."

That was true.

"I'll tell you next time, I promise. He was kissing two girls one night in front of you. You saw, and you never said a word. I figured you really didn't want to deal with it."

That was all true too. "Still tell me."

"Okay. I will." She reached forward, giving me a hug. "Okay. I'm off."

I gave her a nod and a wave as she left, then I considered my night.

I did have class tomorrow, but I was restless.

I didn't want to study. I didn't want to do homework. I didn't want to eat. I didn't want to take a bath. I didn't want to watch a movie. I didn't want to go for a run. I didn't want to do anything.

I knew what I wanted to do and I couldn't do that.

You need to eat.

Are you monitoring my thoughts?

I felt your energy. It was pulling to me. What's wrong?

I sighed. *I don't know.*

I do. You need to eat.

Yeah, well, I snapped back at him. *You're not here.*

He was silent again, until, *Do you want me to be?*

Yes.

Wait. Still me.

Shit. Also me.

Damn stupid thoughts. I was on a roll.

Still going. *Are you already in the area?*

I could feel him grinning. *Micaela. I'll never 'just' be in the area if you need to eat me.*

That sounds so wrong when you say it like that.

I'm aware I'm delicious. You don't have to hide that you want to eat me.

Stop talking.

He laughed.

Stop laughing. Me.

I can come to you, if you'd like? I'm not in the 'area,' but I can be.

He'd do that for me?

Rakon will not shut up if I don't.

I forgot you can hear everything.

He was silent, again.

Then, *I'm letting you decide.*

Right. I heaved a deep breath. *Yes.*

And I closed my eyes so tight, because for some reason, that made me feel vulnerable and I didn't know why.

I'll find you.

Okay.

Micaela.

What?

I wasn't busy the way you thought I was busy. I was in a meeting.

Oh—but he was gone. I felt the connection end on his side, and why did that leave me feeling bereft again?

Stupid dragon. Stupid Kieran. Stupid 'needing to eat.' Just stupid, all of it stupid.

I couldn't wait.

17

POST-HALLOWEEN PARTY

"Hey Nadeem, how's it hanging?"

Nikki's hand was on my arm and tightened as Brad came over to us. We'd just arrived, and Cary, one of Brad's friends, was handing over our drinks. All of us paused at Brad's arrival. His hair was messed up. His shirt was half-ripped and hanging off him. He was wearing red shorts, and he was all sweaty.

He had a sneer when he greeted me, but the sneer turned to a leer as he gave Nikki a once-over. He opened his mouth—

I beat him to the punch. "Thanks for the party invite, Uncle Cream."

His mouth snapped shut, and he glowered at me.

Nikki coughed, clearing her throat. "Okay. We're already off to a great start."

Brad was looking at our outfits.

Nikki came straight from Bass, so she looked hot.

Me, I was wearing a white dress that had a tie behind my neck. I paired that with thigh-high suede hooker boots. I wasn't normally a hooker boots kind of energist, but Kieran was coming and sue me. The girl inside of me wanted to look nice.

We'd be having creature-spirit energy sex, so yeah... Hooker boots felt appropriate. The suede classed them up so they were high-end hooker boots. Also, I wanted an excuse to wear them. Nikki was right.

That last year, Jay and I had only been roommates. The year before, we were barely friends. The beginning two years were good, but it'd been a dying relationship long ago. I never wanted to wear these for Jay.

He never earned that privilege.

"It's a Halloween party. You guys were supposed to dress up."

Nikki smiled at Brad, her hand running down his chest as she moved closer to him. "I did dress up, for you."

She had her head tipped up. His was tipped down.

They'd normally be a cute couple if one wasn't nicknamed Uncle Cream.

"What's wrong, Nadeem? All this for Jay? Don't know if you can compete with his new vamp."

"What?" I frowned.

No. I glared.

Nikki stiffened at Brad's words and pushed backwards, giving them space. "What?"

"Them?" I asked Nikki, not glaring at her.

She was glaring too, at Brad. "What are you talking about?"

"Them. He's here. With her."

"Why didn't you say anything?"

He shrugged. "Why you all pissy about it? Chill. I didn't invite them. The vamp bitch is friends with someone here, and Jay came in with them. I haven't talked to them either, but he was all over her. Figured that meant they were together."

Nikki cursed at him before giving him her back and looking at me. "You okay?"

Kieran.

I hadn't meant to reach out to him, but it was there.

He didn't answer.

Nice.

Are you okay?

This was dumb. I shouldn't have called out to him.

Yeah. I'm fine. Just hungry.

He was quiet again, and there was the connection.

I could feel him inside of me, and he was searching me.

What vampire is with him?

I felt his alarm. It was piqued, but he was keeping it at bay.

How was I feeling his feelings so easily now?

I don't know her name, but it's the same one he cheated on me with. Brad wouldn't have said it if it wasn't true.

There's other vampires there?

I don't know. Why are you getting alarmed?

He was quiet, again.

Then, a roar from his end. That was Rakon.

Kieran?!

It's fine. Leave the party, just in case. I'm almost to you.

Almost? What?

My internal voice was hitching up in my own panic. It was clouding all around me now.

Leave the party? Man. I didn't know about that. Nikki wanted to come for me, but also for her too. She was studying me, and she reached out. "What do you want to do? You want to leave?"

"What?" Brad groaned behind her. His hands went up to his hair, raking through both sides. "Come on. Deal with it. That relationship was a shitshow for the last two years—"

"Shut up!" Nikki whipped around to him, her hand on her hip.

He did, but it was taking effort.

Cary was still standing with us, holding onto his own drink.

He gave me a pitying look, before nodding to Nikki and Brad. "I need to check the kitchen for more cups. Wanna come help?"

"Gladly."

Kieran's warning echoed in my head, but I would leave. In a few.

I glanced back over my shoulder as I was following Cary to the kitchen. Nikki was watching and she mouthed to me, *Are you okay?*

I nodded, giving her a thumbs-up. I mouthed back, *I'll be fine.*

She frowned at that.

I gave her a second thumbs-up, switching my drink to my free hand.

She rolled her eyes, but grinned.

Brad moved in, his arm going around her from the front and he pulled her back to him. He tipped his head to see her, and hers moved to look up at him. He was tugging her backwards when we rounded the corner into the kitchen.

That's when I saw Jay and *her.*

He had his arm around her shoulder, and seeing me, he dropped it real quick.

Real. Quick.

He straightened up from the counter he'd been leaning back against. "Hey, Cale. I never thought I'd see you here." His eyes trailed behind me. "You and Brad are friends?"

Jay was cute.

He'd always been cute. He had a baby-type face with soft brown eyes, and he'd been tall and lanky. He was popular, athletic, and he had an affectionate smile. He was kind. That's what made me fall for him. He hung out with the popular assholes, but not him. They were mean to someone and he told them to shut up. They never turned on him. They respected him.

Jay was the exception to so many of our rules. He was human, and he knew all about us.

Like I said, he'd been the exception.

We began dating, and I was proud to have him as my boyfriend in college.

He held my hand, walked me to my dorm room.

He met me on campus. We ate together.

He used to have his arm around my shoulder too.

But seeing him now, he wasn't the guy I was thinking of.

That told me everything.

So, instead, I turned to her. "You got your orders from Quesadilla to stay with him too?"

Her mouth dropped, and before she could stop herself, her fangs were out.

Now!

That was me, yelling in my head, because I hadn't known I was going to do this, but I did now.

And. It. Was. Awesome.

I felt my creature pushing to let loose, and just as Jay's vamp girlfriend sprang toward me, her two other vampire friends coming to help her, there was an energy explosion in the room.

They didn't see it.

I did.

And I was smiling the whole time because I flung my arms out, my drink went in the air, and I let her loose.

She spread through my body in a flash and this time, we were one. I saw through her eyes. I felt her hunger, but I felt her thirst for power. We went into their energy, and we yanked hard. We didn't eat it, but we could harness it, and as we touched their energy, their bodies started seizing.

You have no energy, you have nothing.

This was my superpower.

I was hungry, so hungry.

I was starving.

They weren't enough.

I needed more—I began looking behind me for more vampires. Anyone who would want to fight me. I took one step, their energy vibrating around me. I was almost levitating, but I felt fangs slice through my skin.

I screamed, the pain and invasion coursing through me.

I reached back, but the vampire was stronger than me.

I tried yanking her energy, but she was draining me too fast.

She. Her.

I recognized her energy, and as I couldn't hold onto my own, the energy slipped from my control. They returned back to the vampires, and as I turned, falling to the ground, my eyes locked with hers.

She was standing there, my blood dripping from her mouth and she wiped at it with the back of her hand. She considered it, then stuck a finger back into her mouth and sucked my blood clean.

She smiled down at me. "Remember me?"

Jay's vamp was moving in fast. Her foot was in the air.

It was coming down on me.

I had one second to think.

Quesadilla is alive!

18

QUESADILLA BITCH

I woke to a headache and a thought. This was the second Halloween night she ruined.

Bitch.

My second thought, I hurt like a bitch.

I couldn't move, not even an inch.

"Tsk, tsk. She wakes."

I recognized that voice, and growled. Or wanted to growl.

I would've growled if I had the energy, and speaking of irony.

"You took my energy."

"I did." She sounded so smug, coming to stand above me.

I was becoming more oriented.

She had me strapped to a table, my legs and arms tied down and something over my neck to hold me in place. I felt something warm and sticky all over my body, and judging by the blood on her face, I was guessing it wasn't her blood.

"I drained you dry, and you were so sweet." She closed her eyes, looking almost blissful. "An energist's blood is like honey from heaven. Now I'm going to do what I do to all my other energy bunnies." She moved, reached out of eyesight, and came back with a syringe. "I drained you, now I'm going to drug you so I can do it all over again. Wouldn't want you to be able to drain my energy, now would we?"

A moan came from somewhere in the room.

"Who's that?"

"Cale." That whimper was Nikki.

I struggled against my restraints. I had enough energy for that. "Let me out!"

"I have your whole group here."

A punching sound, and another groan. This one was deeper.

"Fucking whore," was spat out.

That was Brad.

"They all fought for you."

Brad did?

Quesadilla went on. "It was a valiant effort, but they were outnumbered."

"Cale, I'm so sorry."

Slap!

That'd been Jay.

Quesadilla was looking back down on me. She must've seen my confusion. "Even the ex fought for you." She knelt down, her nail drawing a line down my arm, blood seeping from it.

It wasn't painful. That's how far gone I was.

"You and Dragon Lord screwed up. You drained me. He beheaded me. You burned my body, but I wasn't dead. You missed about fifty other vampires I have."

I narrowed my eyes.

I was trying to summon some fight in me, but I had none. I'd used it all up fighting against my restraints when I heard Nikki's whimper.

"Are they all here now?"

Some of the cockiness faded. Some. Not all. "Why do you want to know that?" She was raising her head up, a hungry look coming over her face. Her tongue cleaned one of her fangs, and she was eyeing the fleshy part of my arm that she just cut.

I felt the earth rumbling.

Was I the only one?

It didn't matter.

I felt him coming.

No, no.

I felt *them* coming.

I was rumbling.

The table I was on was rumbling.

The room was rumbling.

Quesadilla lowered her head, her fangs sinking into my arm. She was oblivious.

I heard things rattling in the room.

Something shattered.

There were curses.

"What the hell?"

A pounding of feet. A door was slammed open. "We have incoming."

Quesadilla moaned, grasping my arm and holding me tighter to her mouth. She was sucking me dry.

Where are you?

Kieran was Rakon. They were one, and chills went through me.

Quesadilla was going to die tonight.

I felt Kieran's darkness.

I could see it in the air. It was filling the room, being sent ahead of him. He was looking for me, and once he found me, that energy filled the entire room up. It was coming over me, covering me.

It was moving over my body.

I felt it licking my body, like a dog would lick a hurt paw.

He was trying to heal me, or his energy was.

Another ferocious roar sounded in my head, but I heard it too. It shook the entire room. There was more stampeding happening.

A door crashed open again. "We have to go. Now!"

"What's happening?"

"Fucking Kieran Raoul is happening. He's coming for her."

"What?!"

A vampire came up behind Quesadilla, who was still drinking from me, and reached for her shoulder.

No! I barked at her in my head.

I didn't know if she heard me, or she just felt me, but she hesitated—and that was enough.

It was Jay's fuck-friend.

She was studying me, and whatever she saw had her whispering, "Oh God. He's your mate, isn't he?"

"What?"

"What?!" from inside the room.

Both were from vampires, or I was guessing vampires, that I didn't know.

"WHAT?!" That was Nikki.

"Who's he?" Jay.

"Shit." Uncle Cream. "What's everyone going on about?"

There was another roar, and this one shook everyone. Jay's bitch trembled before she raised her head, turning to face away.

He was here.

I felt him.

In a blink, he swooped in and everyone was gone.

Jay's bitch.

Quesadilla.

It was silence. An eerie silence.

A third roar, but from farther away.

"Oh my God. He's eating them." Nikki sounded anguished.

"That's one way to kill 'em."

I sighed. Brad. Of course.

There was more screaming.

People or whoever was running.

"He's coming back."

I didn't know who said that, but I felt them.

They swooped over us, Kieran and Rakon's shadow like a quick blink of the eye, and there were more screams.

It was the screams. The sound of terror.

I felt their energy.

It was all being drained down to me.

I was so drained, so weak.

I didn't want to taste what they felt, but I couldn't not. I needed to eat. I was too weak otherwise—*Do not!*

I need to eat.

No. Me. That's it. No one else.

Kieran...

I was so hungry. So tired. So exhausted.

I can't—

You will! Two more sweeps and I have them all. Hold on. Just, hold on.

He did two more sweeps, and I ignored the energy that was dancing around me. I was almost frothing with drool. I was so hungry, but I held on.

I waited.

Until there was silence.

Someone was crying. Nikki.

Someone was weeping. I didn't know who.

"This shit is insane." A whisper from Brad.

A deep thud, and I felt Kieran coming to me.

I was able to move my head, and there he was.

He was looking at me through Rakon's eyes.

I thought, *You're beautiful.*

He was all black, with the points of his scales tinted in blue.

His eyes were large and oval, a literal fire inside of them. His body was the size of three football fields. He had blown the house away, so when he walked over, I felt a chill in the air. He seemed to sense this and his head lowered, his breath coming out to coat me like a warm blanket.

He moved to see me more squarely. *Are you okay?*

I'm hungry.

But it was more.

If our creatures were mates, or we were mates, I didn't know. I didn't care at this point. I needed him.

He blinked, understanding there. *Trust me, okay?*

I closed my eyes. *Yes.*

A muffled scream came from someone just as I felt more of his hot breath, then his teeth were nudging at my restraints. They came undone. I think one melted under his fire, which only teased at my skin, before I felt his teeth moving over me.

He was scraping me gently.

What are you doing?

Testing your injuries.

"What are you doing to her?"

Kieran ignored them, continuing with my restraints.

He freed my legs.

He was moving to my arm when Nikki yelled, "Hey! I don't care who you are, if you hurt her—"

Kieran whipped his head around, flames breathing out from his nostrils. *You'll do what?*

I had enough energy to look more around, and I saw Nikki shrink backwards.

I knew his voice had gotten inside her head.

"Nik," I whispered.

Her large eyes moved to mine. I saw her standing in a cage. Where the cage came from, I hadn't a clue, but she fell down seeing me seeing her. Her hands were wrapped tightly around the bars.

"I'm okay."

He freed my second arm, and he opened his giant mouth over me.

"He's going to eat you," she whispered back.

"No."

His jaws closed over me, but he only lifted me from the table.

I was secure in his mouth. Nothing was hurting anymore.

I was tuned into him and Rakon. Both were worried about me.

He was about to lift off again.

I said to Nikki right before he did, "Trust me. I'll be back."

He sprang up, and we were soaring. Going higher and higher.

I was flying.

19

YES

When I woke, I was warm all over, and I felt like I was levitating. I wasn't. I moved around, and I felt blankets underneath me, but that was the feeling in my body. I felt 'light' all over.

In a flash, the night came back to me.

The post-Halloween party.

Uncle Cream.

Going into the kitchen.

Jay and her.

Quesadilla.

Quesadilla's fangs.

Blood.

Nothing.

Waking, feeling lower than absolute shit.

Threats.

Grossness.

More Quesadilla's fangs.

And then, Kieran.

So much Kieran.

All hot and sexy things Kieran.

I felt a rumble inside of me and instantly thought, *Sorry, Rakon.*

I amended my earlier memories to: Rakon, Rakon, Rakon.

Better.

I felt him leaving again, feeling happy.

I bolted upright, my heart pounding.

I just felt Rakon's emotions.

Rakon's.

I only got glimpses of Kieran's emotions before, but not Rakon's and not this strong. Everything was more, all more.

I felt the bed beneath me.

I felt the air around me.

I felt the particles in the air.

I could hear a buzzing in the air and looked out a window. I was hearing the electrical wires, a mile away. I was seeing the wires, a mile away. Through trees, down a hill.

I knew it all and felt it all, and I was having a heart attack.

What was happening to me?

"You merged with your creature last night."

Kieran was leaning against the doorframe, regarding me.

I had no clue what that meant.

One side of his mouth curved up. He straightened from the doorframe and began to move toward me. "That means you're not separated anymore. You're a complete energist." He sat on the edge of the bed.

It dipped underneath him and those dark eyes were assessing me.

He asked, "How do you feel?"

"I feel good."

I moved, and nope. There was an ache there, a big ache.

I groaned, and Kieran grinned again. "You were saying?"

I moved back, sighing. "I'm hurting. Never mind."

"Your body went through a trauma last night and you merged. I'd imagine you'll feel sore for a day."

"Only a day?"

He nodded, his gaze sweeping over me. "A day. At least. You fed a little on me last night, enough to start the merge, but not enough to fill you."

"Oh."

I didn't remember feeding.

"You were exhausted. I made you eat a little before you fell asleep."

I was disappointed. I'd been looking forward to eating him.

His gaze lifted, then falling to my mouth. "That's the plan for today."

Right.

He could hear me. I kept forgetting.

"You choose to forget."

Right on that too.

He smirked.

Right. Again.

"Sorry."

He shook his head. "No. It's entertaining."

"So, you and Rakon, huh?"

A faint smile from him. "Once Rakon felt you were hurting, there was no stopping him. He rose on his own, and he never does that."

Mate.

We both heard him and shared a smile.

"There's that, huh?"

His eyes met mine, staying. Growing somber. "Right."

A pressure was building inside of me.

I felt like I was going to burst, so I did what every normal person would do.

I changed the subject. "Where does Rakon usually stay?"

It was a question every supernatural being knew about because dragons were the top of the chain. It was also known that there was an under-universe, like the flipside of our surface of another world. Dragons lived there. I thought it'd all been a fantasy story, until I found out Kieran existed.

"Do other dragons live there?"

He nodded. "Rakon's the only one that's merged with a sire."

It was another reminder how ancient, and how powerful Kieran was.

I'd never felt smaller.

He grinned, but taunted me. *Scared?*

I laughed, my voice hitching on an uncomfortable note. *Maybe.*

I don't blame you. It's taken me a bit to admit it myself.

"Really?" My lips parted in surprise.

He nodded, his gaze returning to my mouth. "I felt it. As soon as I felt your energy in the area, I knew who you were to me. Then you came to me, and I found out you were sent by Quessadiline, and I was furious. I wasn't accepting you, what you were to me, and you didn't seem to know yourself."

I remembered that first night in the blue velvet room. "Uh, I felt something that night, just thought it was a side effect to you analyzing me."

A full smile came from him. "No. Most aren't aware of me 'analyzing' them. That reaction was a mate reaction."

That word again.

"You don't seem happy about that." I was going out on a limb here, my heart was picking up, pounding harder.

His eyes flicked up to mine, but returned just as quick to my mouth.

He spoke, but he did it very quietly. "I've not had a mate for three centuries. It's...an unusual feeling to have again." He looked away. "And there's changes that need to be made."

Changes.

Unusual feeling.

He so wasn't happy about it.

I sat up, bringing my knees up and I wrapped my arms around them. I hugged them to my chest, propping my chin on top of one. "Nothing has to change, you know. I mean, Rakon said my creature was his mate—" I stopped at the look Kieran gave me. "What?"

"You are your creature now. When we brought you back here, Rakon claimed you."

"What do you mean by that?"

"He breathed on you. The mating mark surfaced over you, that's what helped merge you and your creature together."

I—I have no idea what to think about that.

You know about mate marks.

I did, but they were almost as mythical as Kieran himself. It was an age-old belief that was believed to be, well, in the ages.

"Where is it?"

"On your back."

"I don't remember that."

"You had passed out."

"Is that why I'm hurting?"

He shook his head. "Mate marks don't hurt. Do you want to see it?"

I nodded. Oh boy, did I.

He came over, and he bent down. His arms slid under me, and whoosh, he picked me up.

I squawked from the suddenness of the action, my arms going around him in reflex.

Most of it was reflex. Some of it. I was totally melting on the inside all over again.

Kieran's gaze moved to mine, and he stayed there, watching me as he carried me into his bathroom.

He set me on the vanity and stood between my legs. Still holding my gaze, his hands moved to my shirt. I was in a tanktop, and he pushed up the bottom, lifting it up and over me. I was still in my bra from last night.

His gaze trailed behind me.

I looked back, and gasped.

It was beautiful.

A full winding dragon stretched over my entire back. The edges were detailed and looked as if the dragon was on fire. Its mouth was raised toward my neck, open, and it looked as if fire itself was rising upwards.

"That came because he breathed on me?"

His hand flexed next to my leg. "That and because we held you in our mouth when we flew you here. The combination of both."

I'd never seen something as beautiful as that mark, and I felt an underlying pulsating inside of me. As if feeling it too, Kieran moved closer into me, his voice coming out rough, "That's Rakon. He can feel you."

I lifted my eyes in the mirror, seeing Kieran looking at me and the intensity in his eyes stole that breath from my throat. I almost gasped, but then Kieran turned to the mirror and his eyes found mine there. There was a fierce emotion mixing with his intensity and a warmth was spreading inside of me, just from seeing it.

My heart began beating even harder.

"Do you want to feel your mark?"

I nodded. I so very badly wanted to touch it.

"Touch it through me." He raised his hand, as if asking for my permission, and I nodded again.

He leaned closer, his breath coating my shoulder as his finger touched at the base of the mark first.

A surge of pleasure speared through me, and it only raised as his finger went over every inch of the mark.

I was feeling it through him, but also feeling his touch inside me at the same time.

Is it always like this?

His head had lowered closer to my shoulder and I felt his breath caress me. *I've only had one other mate, but this is more than what I remember.*

I had closed my eyes and I didn't know it until I looked at him. *More?*

He met my gaze, our lips an inch apart. *More.*

Everything beautiful I had ever experienced in my life, all the memories, all the feelings, even the tears of joy, every single one of them happened again. At once. Right now. All together, and I gasped from the onslaught of it all. My throat was choking up.

Kieran... I started, but hesitated.

He kept watching me, but his finger was moving over the mark.

Every curve, turn. The skin raised to make the outline and he went over each peak, even the details to make it look as if it were on fire.

I could see it perfectly through him, his mind.

He was letting me see through him, and I was inside of him because of it.

Did you want a mate?

Some didn't. I would understand if he was one of those.

I didn't when I felt you, no.

I started to look away, but his other hand caught my chin. A lone finger and he turned me to look at him again.

That's changed. I was already coming for you, but when we felt Quessadiline's presence, I called for Rakon without a second thought. He was rising anyways. We both felt it. Rakon has always waited for me. He's never risen without my signal. That's how important you are to him. His hand moved to the back of my neck, spreading out. He cupped me there. *To me. You're ours. You're mine.*

He had moved even closer, our chests were touching.

I almost felt every inch of him, and I closed my eyes, giving in.

A swell flooded me, enveloping me, and taking me.

You haven't eaten enough yet.

I nodded, already answering his call to me. I drew his energy in, digesting it, and it wasn't the same response as the first time. I knew now that I had been pulled into Rakon. This time, it was both of them. My energy was mingling with his, and lust exploded everywhere. Inside of me. Outside of me. In Kieran. Around us. If I'd opened my eyes, I knew I would've seen it in the air surrounding us.

A rough groan left him, and his mouth came to mine.

That made everything even *more*, tenfold more.

I fed from him, and his energy, and when I was done, he lifted me back up. His mouth never left mine, his tongue slipping inside. He took me back to his bed, laying me down, and coming to cover me. He lay gently over me, but I groaned, needing him.

"You're sore—"

I shook my head, my mouth catching him. *Not anymore. I need this.*

His whole body shuddered as he began kissing me back, answering my demand. He took control and demanded from me instead.

I have never felt this before.

I was scared to say the name of what I was feeling, but it was bringing tears to my eyes as Kieran undressed me.

As he kissed me.

As he moved back over me.

As he slid inside of me.

As he filled me.

He was me. We were one.

Humans didn't know what this feeling was. They said it, but they could never experience it. I was inside of Kieran, feeling me through him and he was doing the same. He was thrusting, and the sensations were a continuous wave of pleasure.

This. He said in my head, watching me as he moved inside of me. *You are my mate.*

I watched him back. *Yes,* a whisper back from me.

Yes.

Under my touch on his back, I felt his own dragon mark surface.

20

EXPLAIN YOURSELF

Nikki: Hello? ARE YOU ALIVE?!

Cale: Yes. Sorry. Caught up on stuff. I have some things to tell you.

Nikki: THE HELL YOU DO! OMG FREAKING KIERAN RAOUL? R U KIDDING ME?

Cale: Give me a few more days.

NIKKI: DAYS?! I'M FREAKING OUT HERE. Also, Brad is serious about trying for a relationship. What do you think? I need my girl's input.

Cale: Are you serious? I knew that was the reason for the party, to make up for the shitty Halloween that you had, but ... What are you thinking?

Nikki: I have no idea. None. I need you to come and tell me what his energy is saying.

Cale: Okay. Just hold off. I need a few more days with Kieran and then I'll be back.

Nikki: OMG! KIERAN. I can't. Holy shit, holy

shit, holy shit. He rules the other half of the world, literally.

Cale: Dude. I've not even told you about Rakon.

Nikki: RAKON?!

TWO DAYS LATER.

Nikki: I can't wait any longer. What's going on? I need to know.

Cale: lol I know. There's a lot of changes going on.

Nikki: I can only imagine.

Cale: A few more days?

Nikki: What about your classes?

Cale: I had my last exam. That's getting worked out too.

Nikki: Okay. I miss you. Jay asked about you.

Cale: Jay?

Nikki: He was in the cages with us. He fought for you.

Cale: I had no idea.

Nikki: He's saying he's just concerned about you, about Kieran. He's sniffing, being nosey.

Cale: That's none of his business. How are things with Brad?

Nikki: You're just trying to distract me.

Cale: Yes. Did it work?

Nikki: YES! Now I can only think about Brad. Let's have an actual conversation tomorrow. I'm heading to Bass for a shift. Guess who are being super friendly to me? Trey and EVERYONE. I'm loving it. They're all kissing my ass because of you. Anyways, love you girl. Miss you. I have to babysit Bud tomorrow too, so a phone call would be awesome.

Cale: Yes right back. Grrr to Trey and everyone else. Stay sane with Bud. Follow your gut with Brad. You might have to just try it to get him/it out of your system?

LATER THAT NIGHT.

Nikki: Yeah.

Cale: What?

Nikki: Brad showed up at Bass during one of my breaks...

Cale: You opened your bedsheets for him?

Nikki: I'm weak. We're going to try.

Cale: Now you'll know, though. I'm being supportive for you trying. But, if it goes bad, you'll finally know.

Nikki: I'd rather know more about you and your MATE!

Cale: lol soon. Promise. Love you lady.

Nikki: Love you back.

21

DON'T CALM ME

I CAN FEEL YOUR NERVES.

I didn't spare Kieran a look because I was keenly aware of everything about him. How he was sitting next to me in the back of his vehicle. How he was multitasking by working, having conversations in his head with some of his workers, and how he was now tuning into me. Sometimes I could hear his conversations. He never allowed them in his head, but he'd go into theirs. Some were powerful enough to converse back, others couldn't. I was learning all that out because as an energist, telepathy wasn't one of our skill sets.

At least it wasn't mine until Kieran.

But he was feeling my edginess, and I had a lot going on.

We were on our way back to Bass.

We'd been at Kieran's estate in Indonesia, and it'd been amazing. More than amazing. Overwhelmingly amazing.

Seriously. Very overwhelming.

Kieran and I were still learning about each other, but we were psychically and magically linked. We knew the core of each other and because of that, I could feel his concern for me even before he said anything.

Everything is going to change now.

I could feel the buzz of three conversations he was still having with his employees, but his hand slipped to mine. He gave me a squeeze, and shifted his focus to me.

It'll be fine.

He meant it when he said that, and I felt him pushing some of that reassurance over to me.

Stop.

But I thought that with a grin because I knew he wouldn't.

Within seconds, I was content. The worry was pushed out, and he sent a surge of strength right after.

Nikki and I had our phone conversation, but I wanted to wait for a girl's night before really filling her in on all things Kieran. Because of that, I told her the gist of what happened and how it came to happen, then asked her about Brad. The plan was to head to Bass where Nikki was working her shift.

Everyone knew we were coming, or I was assuming.

Kieran was the new owner, and the workers there knew he was coming. Nikki knew I was coming with him so I was just doing the math here.

Kieran would do what he needed to do and I'd spend my time with Nikki. After that, we were going to figure things out. Whether that was staying here for me or staying where he needed to. I had a feeling we'd be doing a lot of traveling.

I had another feeling that the Western Hemisphere was going to need to get used to seeing a dragon flying around more than it had before. Rakon rose quite a bit when we were at Kieran's, and Kieran shifted and merged with Rakon. All of us went flying after that.

Our time had been almost dream-like.

You're starting to worry again.

It's a big adjustment.

He stopped his other conversations and turned to me. I was getting his whole focus now.

The power and intensity behind his gaze reached all the way inside of me, taking hold of my heart, and it was like he was cradling that in the palm of his hand.

Me too.

What?

Me, too. That's how I've felt about you since my mark showed. You have my heart.

I wasn't going to cry. Nope.

Not going to cry.

Not me.

Micaela.

Sigh. The soft way he thought my name, and I felt it reverberate inside of me. It was like a drum beating and sending the waves of the rhythm outwards.

Kieran.

Mates are for life.

I know.

No, you don't because I can feel your resistance.

He was right, but images were bombarding me.

As he was staring at me, studying me in the blue velvet room.

Our time in his vehicle.

When he stopped at Harry Bahl's for me.

When we eviscerated Quesadilla, the first time.

The time after.

When I was missing him and I didn't want to admit it.

When Rakon reached out to me.

When I thought Kieran was having sex.

When Kieran told me he wasn't having sex.

When he was concerned about me not eating.

When he said he'd come back so I could eat him.

When Quesadilla attacked me.

When I felt them coming for me.

When he killed Quesadilla for me, a second time.

When I woke and felt Rakon's mark on me.

When we kissed.

When he slid inside of me.

When Kieran's matching mate mark surfaced on him.

You're doing this, I thought to him.

He was sending me all those images, but they were memories from his point of view. I was feeling his intrigue, his confusion, his reluctance, his amusement, his interest, his caring, his concern, his warmth towards me, and then his possession, his claim.

The last one had me blinking my eyes.

I knew it. I felt it.

I was scared to label it.

I feel that, too. But I wasn't scared to tell him.

I know.

He squeezed my hand again before leaning over, cupping the back of my head, and kissing me a soft kiss to my forehead. He touched his forehead to mine after, and I looked at him. He was looking at me.

He had shut everyone else out.

We rode like that until we pulled up to Bass.

22

SO GIRLY

We walked into Bass, and all eyes were on us.

All eyes were on Kieran, but then the curiosity and somewhat hostile attention turned to me. I was having deja vu from when we walked into Quesadilla's compound.

This time, it was demons.

And this time, I heard a, "MICAELAAAAAA!" before Nikki broke from the crowd and came running at me.

We ran to each other.

We collided. We didn't care.

Arms around each other.

Bodies hitting each other.

We were laughing, and crying, and being girls.

"Oh, girl! I have missed you so freaking much." Nikki wound her arms even tighter around my neck.

I squeezed her back.

Kieran was inside of me, feeling the hug through our link. He started to pull out, giving us privacy.

No. I pulled him back. I wanted him to feel how I felt about Nikki.

She's a good friend to you.

Except for the part where she didn't tell me Jay was cheating on me.

Well, she's a demon. And that's not an issue anymore.

I glanced back, grinning at him.

He grinned back before the Stuck-Up Vampire from the blue velvet room approached him.

I need to go and work.

Okay.

I was still hugging Nikki. We were starting to rock back and forth.

If you go with her, my driver will take you.

What about--

I stopped in mid-thought because I knew. His driver would take me to Nikki's apartment. He'd return for Kieran, and both of them would come to get me.

Kieran would take me back to the estate he uses here.

Nikki just didn't know that part.

Your friend understands mates. She's expecting it.

You're in her head?

She was worried about you. She's not so much anymore. Have fun with your friend. I'll come for you tonight.

After that thought, I felt his own surge of emotions. Possession. Need. Want.

And that emotion I was still scared to label.

I felt him walking away, his mind returning to his other conversations from before.

"I get you tonight, don't I?"

Nikki pulled back, asking as she did.

I heard the uncertainty in her voice, and guilt speared me a moment.

I didn't like hearing that in my best friend.

I nodded. "Yes. Your place?"

She laughed, the relief palpable in her tone. "Hell yeah! Ralph ubered me here. I was told that I should expect to ride back with Kieran Raoul's mate because he's not likely to let her ride back unattended." She rolled her eyes upwards, grinning. "I'm lying. I wasn't told that, but anyone who's anyone in our world would know that about you."

We headed out.

I felt Kieran through our link, and I felt his goodbye.

I sent mine back, linked arms with Nikki and we were getting into our vehicle.

"Fancy schmancy." Nikki climbed in, looking all around.

It was the same vehicle I rode in with Kieran to Quesadilla's compound. I hadn't taken it in on that ride. I'd been worried about Nikki and distracted by Kieran, but since then I'd come to appreciate the grandiose of it.

Leather seats.

Blacked-out windows.

There was a whole system where we could push a button, and our drink of choice would roll out. I used it for coffee one time.

Then a latte.

Then a chai tea.

An espresso.

"So." Nikki's head was relaxing all the way back. She was watching me. "Do you love him?"

My heart skipped a beat.

I felt Kieran fully through our link now.

You're eavesdropping.

About this? Fuck yes, I am.

I smiled. "Do you love Brad?"

Nikki's mouth dropped. "Are you serious? We talked about Brad already. Brad is like old bread by now. He's old news, even though I love bread and I'll always love bread. You and Kieran

Raoul. Everyone is talking about it. Him having a mate? And him having a mate in our hemisphere? That's the only thing people are talking about. Or, not people. You know what I mean."

I felt a nudge from Kieran.

Well?

I nudged him right back, answering, "Yes. I do."

I could feel him smiling. *I love you, too.*

We were mates so fast.

Everything happened so fast, but I did.

I loved him.

This is just the beginning, Micaela.

I know.

I was brought back to the vehicle because Nikki was squealing, grasping my arm, and she was kicking her feet a little. I waited a second, then I joined in because this was a moment that I needed to be all girly about.

———————

It was later that night, after Nikki had passed out when I felt Kieran coming for me.

I knew he had business to handle and I was tired so I went into the guest room, but I was awake.

He came in, and bent over me.

His arms slid underneath me.

I was waiting for you.

He tucked me against his chest and turned back for the door.

I'm glad you did.

He took me to his house, and he told me all over again how he loved me.

He showed me too.

23

HALLOWEEN

TEN YEARS LATER.

"Go on." I nudged Raki forward, nodding to the doorbell. "Ring the doorbell."

He looked up at me, Kieran's eyes and my father's chin. "You do it, Mom." He pressed back into my legs.

"Oh my God! I'll do it." Drakaina was the opposite of her brother.

Same age. Same eyes. Same hair.

Completely different personalities. Also, she had my chin.

She pushed forward and jammed her little finger into the doorbell.

There was a stampede coming for the door.

The doorknob was being fumbled with, then it was swept open.

Nikki stood there, holding her one year old on a hip. The screen door was opened, and their Mickayla ran straight for Drakaina. Both girls collided, arms around each other, and the squealing began.

"Come to my room! See the mural that Buddy drew for me."

"Okay!"

Both took off, and Nikki stepped back. Her eyes were on me before falling to Raki. "Hey, little man. How's it going?"

Raki melted for Nikki, every single time. His cheeks got red and he folded his head down, his little finger curling even tighter around mine. He mumbled to the floor, "Hi, Aunt Nikki."

She was melting right back for him, fanning herself as she mouthed to me, *So cute.*

I know, I mouthed right back.

She knelt down, shifted Bradley further up and whispered to Raki, who was leaning towards her now, "There's some candy on the table, if you want to have first pick. Don't tell the girls."

He giggled, glanced up at me. I nodded, and he took off.

Nikki stood back up, and we were hugging.

"I've missed you."

I said it right back, "Missed you more."

I reached for little Bradley. It was my godmother's right.

He came, laughing and gleeing. Then he reared back, his eyes shuddered black and he smacked both my cheeks together. If he could squeeze my face together, he would.

"He's his father's kid."

Nikki laughed, shutting the door behind us. "He sure is. You ready for some trick-or-treating?"

Kieran and I lived most of the year in the Eastern Hemisphere. The other third part of the year, we were here.

We always made sure we were here for Halloween.

I used to think that first one sucked so bad.

Now, it was the best one. It's where I met my Big Bad.

I told you it was just the beginning. From Kieran.

You did. When are you done for the night?

As soon as you're ready for me.

Okay. Love you.

Love you.

And from Rakon, *Love you.*

I smiled.

I hope you enjoyed my novella!
If you did, please leave a review. They help so much.
For more stories, and more stories to come:
www.tijansbooks.com

ACKNOWLEDGMENTS

I mostly want to thank the ladies in my reader group! I did a poll and asked if they wanted paranormal or not. They chose paranormal, and it was so much fun to write. I haven't written paranormal in so long, but I have a feeling there might be more coming from me.

Thank you to Debra Anastasia and Helena Hunting. We wanted to do our Halloween novellas together. Out of sheer stubbornness, we made it happen.

Thank you to Crystal, Amy, Eileen, and the rest of my editing and proofreading team. I've been in all of your messages a lot lately, and you guys always make the time for myself and my projects. I truly appreciate it.

Last, I hope everyone has/had a great Halloween. Let yourself believe in a little magic.

ALSO BY TIJAN

Paranormal:

Evil (standalone)

Davy Harwood Series (paranormal)

Sports Romance Standalones:

Enemies

Teardrop Shot

Hate To Love You

Rich Prick

The Not-Outcast

Series:

Fallen Crest Series

Crew Series

Broken and Screwed Series (YA/NA)

Jaded Series (YA/NA suspense)

Carter Reed Series (mafia)

The Insiders Trilogy

Mafia Standalones:

Cole

Bennett Mafia

Canary

Young Adult Standalones:

Ryan's Bed

A Whole New Crowd

Brady Remington Landed Me in Jail

College Standalones:

Antistepbrother

Kian

Contemporary Romances:

The Boy I Grew Up With (standalone)

Bad Boy Brody

Home Tears

Fighter

Nate

Rockstar Romance Standalone:

Sustain

And more to come!

.

CPSIA information can be obtained
at www.ICGtesting.com
Printed in the USA
FSHW010015191020
74935FS